PURGE SEQUENCE

I0593851

CURVE

OF

HUMANITY

BOOK THREE

MAQUEL A. JACOB

Cover art by:

Keith Johnston

https://keithdraws.wordpress.com

Edited by:

Rhiannon Rhys-Jones

Published by MAJart Works

www.majartworks.com

Hillsboro, Oregon

ISBN: 978-0-9979564-5-0

ACKNOWLEDGEMENTS

Thank you for taking a chance on my new six book series Curve of Humanity. My great passion is to find the good in humanity and show we can combat corruption within our societies. This book series is a lesson of hope in the face of futility.

Or so I would like to think.

For those who encouraged me to keep going when it all seemed too daunting, I appreciate you all. To the early stage beta readers and Mom, my sincere condolences and immense gratitude. Your enthusiasm and no holds barred feedback is priceless.

A huge thanks to NaNoWriMo (National Novel Writing Month) for supporting writers' creative juices. My peeps at NIWA, you all keep my humble and showed me to put myself out there with no fear.

Sarah Walker and John Howard, two awesome writing buddies who helped hone my craft.

To Sunni and Jason V. Brock for making me turn the dial in my brain and retrain it. Thank you, William F. Nolan for constantly telling me not to quit; to keep writing and keep learning.

Keith Johnston: Your talent is mind blowing. I never thought the covers would turn out so awesome. Look forward to working with you again on future projects.

CHAPTER ONE

A Sonnet for Humanity

-Blind Sheep-

I had hope for some sense of sanity
It being the 21st century of man
But, it seems we are losing our humanity
With no way of fixing it- If we can.
The end is near, or so they say
They, being the prophets and pessimists
Salivating at the promise of doomsday
Even as society and everyday life persists.
Let us not fall in line
Marching towards our own annihilation
And read into the inevitable sign
Of our final destination
Lest we forget an important note
We all wear the same human coat.

- Rachel E. Robinson 2012

ESTABLISHED LAWS

Agent X grimaced at the data on the three holoscreens before him. He sat in a dark panic room surrounded by tiny lights flickering from the electronics on the walls that reflected onto his glass desk. As one of the few Shadow observers still active, he hated the way things had turned out. He used to be a renowned super spy decades ago. Now he was completely off the grid, a mere shadow himself. His assigned territory was basically a warzone, depending on who you talked to. The inner city was divided in two sections; the Relliant aliens not interested in the upcoming war, and the humans who despised them regardless.

Prejudice and bigotry were the staple of every society. No one should've been surprised when human decency went out the window despite the arrival of aliens. The status of hybrid humans was still heatedly debated, and after the scientists created those damnable facilities governments followed suit with more of their own. Then General Perrara and Professor Makoto established the Shadow Organization, bringing about a new mess of social unacceptance for mankind to face.

Laser fire streaked the air while remnants of pipe bombs polluted the streets and he could do nothing except watch. A muffled sound nearby made him grab the long armed electric zapper leaning against the desk's edge. Without taking his eyes off the screen, he jabbed the large sack laying at his feet. Out of the corner of his

1

eye, he watched the bag twitch and convulse then go still. A message notification popped up in the bottom of the middle screen and he clicked it using a mouse.

EXTRACTION REQUIRED.

Nothing followed. He sighed and typed a reply.

WHERE?

MIDWEST. INDIANA.

That shithole.

One of the worst regions to date was the great Heartland of America, the Midwest. Every so often he would get a request from there and he hated leaving his protected nest. He typed his response.

NEED TO TIE UP LOOSE ENDS. TIMELINE?

THREE DAYS. The other party answered.

DONE.

Having seen enough of the street fighting, he turned off the screens. Soft, overhead lighting came on as he swiveled around in his chair and leaned down closer to the sack. He pulled the string and yanked the fabric open to reveal a hog tied thirty something white male. An old sock peeked out from the corner of the strip tape covering his mouth. Agent X preferred old school tactics lately, feeling nostalgic. From the desk drawer, he brought out a small taser and zapped the man.

His hostage jolted from the shock and his eyes flew open. Agent X slapped him hard to make sure he stayed conscious. Hatred stared back at him. Agent X let out a small laugh. Sometimes, he wished he could call on one of the Shadow elite to come do a number on his captives. Of course, if he did that, he would need to splatter proof his entire safehouse.

"I got your attention? Good. You're going to tell me what I want to know. I have other business to attend to."

The man's stare didn't waver. Agent X could see his hands trying to get out of the fiber mesh ropes. It would do no good. That rope was specially made to be unbreakable. Alien input for the advancement of technology brought about a few decent inventions. He rummaged through his desk and found the boning knife he kept for such interrogations. This time the man's eyes went wide with astonishment.

"Barbaric, right? But, since you're being difficult, we'll do it this way."

Agent X stood, towering over the captive, his expression turning dark.

Yes, nostalgia was good.

～

Section seventeen of the new Person's Rights bill clearly stated it was unlawful to imprison, torture, experiment on, or murder a Bi-Genetic unless authorized through a sanctioned government entity. Even that left a bad taste in the President of the United States's mouth. Every country had adopted the same law with similar wording. It exposed the various loopholes regarding enforcement. Her interpretation of it was unpopular with some of the scientists who she couldn't give two fucks about, not after the decades of horrors they committed. So many regular humans were still reeling from the existence of half aliens. The dawn of a new age of man came with growing pains.

She herself had a teenage son with the predisposition to be female. As he got older, she struggled mentally on how to deal if he decided to go with that option. All four of her children were boys and to suddenly have a daughter after eighteen years would throw her entire family for a loop.

In a navy pantsuit and her hair in a traditional bun, she paced the Oval Office. The only room in the White House left alone in design and function, minus the new inconspicuously installed surveillance equipment. She waited, arms crossed, dreading the new crime reports due out today. Per her instructions, it was now mandatory to bring them to her before public release.

The Secretary of Homeland Security entered quickly without knocking and slammed the door shut on the secret service agents that followed him. His long strides stopped less than a foot from her. The tablet in his hand seemed to scream from his grip and his red rimmed eyes showed disdain.

"Is it really that bad, George?" She asked him.

"Why? Why are we our own worst enemy?" George responded angrily. "The Karysilans are probably changing their minds on helping us. And I don't blame them one bit."

President Lynmore unfolded one arm and let it hang. She stood still for a moment, wondering the same thing. Assumptions that humans would adapt and evolve as one race like others in the galaxy were proofing false.

"Let me see it," she demanded, reaching for his tablet. He reluctantly obliged. She scrolled through the data, her face tightening with each entry. "It's way better than the last few years but still disheartening."

George sighed. He sat down on the sofa and let his head fall back. A tall man at six feet seven inches, he was a former basketball player who went to a prestigious university and earned a PhD in Social Economics. He always handled himself with pride and conviction. This new era found him being tested at every turn.

"I think we should re-evaluate our agreement with the aliens. If they decide to back out, we're screwed." His gaze never left the ceiling.

"Is Darnizva still hanging around on Earth?" Then she frowned. "Or do you mean those others who are doing God knows what with that so called secret organization we're supposed to know nothing about?"

George snorted and lifted his head to look at her.

"At least they're trying something."

"It's a roaring mess."

"Well, I heard a little chirp about something new in the wings. If it goes well," he said, cutting himself short. The President gave him a quizzical look. "Let's just say we may have a shot at winning this thing in terms of manpower."

"So, I should turn a blind eye for now?"

"For now," he replied with a dark expression.

She saw right then how much of a leash he would give the Shadow Organization from there.

The mountain bunker's floor to ceiling windows let in full sunlight, enhancing the glorious view of the forest below. On the upper level sat the sleek, modern communal room, sparsely furnished with every piece of equipment the latest technology. In addition to the female Estelarian warrior now known as Celestial Mother, her mate, and the two Chombrazens males, Captain Darnizva lounged in a giant egg chair deep in thought. He had summoned for help in training the humans and, after seeing the outcome, regretted his decision.

As if reading his mind, Celestial Mother turned away from the window to stare at him. Her dark golden hair was like a lion's mane that hung down her back. The equally honey colored eyes bore down on every living thing as a nemesis. In an all-white jumpsuit, she was nothing close to angelic.

"My fledgling Captain," she cooed. He winced at the term. "This is not going well."

"I understand your frustration," Darnizva said.

"Do you?" Karias asked.

His voice boomed more than usual.

"I beg you, don't abandon them yet."

"Oh, Darnizva, they have already done that them-selves," Celestial Mother replied.

He could only nod, having already evacuated his entire human bloodline off the planet. There was much protest, so he had them put in cryochambers and sent off to a neutral zone within the galaxy. Leaving his family in the hands of human government agencies was no longer an option. The only good thing was the scientists hadn't dared touch them for fear of retaliation.

"The timeline is fast approaching," Darnizva stated.

"Indeed." She walked across the room towards him, taking only three steps to do it. "I think we can remedy the situation," she paused, "if they prove more willing."

Darnizva's mood darkened. The female alien was notorious for playing dangerous games when it came to humans. He would not tolerate whatever she had in mind. Standing, he came face to face, eye to eye, with her. They searched each other's intentions silently.

"Do you wish to challenge me?" Celestial Mother asked. "Youngling."

In a flash of light, swords clashed together and a com-petition of might between them began, their eyes never leaving the other's through the gap where the blades intersected. Her mate jumped from his seat to defend her. The two Chombrazen grabbed him by the shoulders and pulled him back down.

Celestial Mother roared and pushed harder. Darnizva held steady, not budging. He pushed back, his rage on the verge of unleashing when suddenly he felt her stop. His own eyes reflected in hers and he saw the glow of red. She stepped back in what appeared to be fear, then it was gone.

"Let's not play today, shall we?" She asked sweetly yet he could hear…trepidation?

"Fine." He sheathed his weapon, as did she. "Don't put anymore strain on this race than they already have. They are fragile creatures compared to us."

Celestial Mother waved the notion away with one hand and turned back to the view of the valley below. Darnizva let the knot in his stomach relax. He had never claimed to be humanity's champion, but they needed one. And he still blamed himself.

⌒

Hana hated the necessity of bureaucracy. Six protective agencies representatives sat in his conference room looking bent out of shape about Bi-Genetics being extracted without their consent. They had been put in place at the height of the facilities and Hana had no love for them. He snorted out loud, getting their attention for the wrong reasons. Those government entities protected no one. All a sham, in his opinion. More sin and atrocity happened in those places than anywhere else.

The Child and Welfare representative cleared her throat. Hana gave her an evil look and she flinched before speaking.

"There was an incident in Indiana that we cannot condone. The family was physically assaulted to the point of being incapacitated and the child was drugged before removal."

Hana's eyebrows shot up in amusement. "Oh?"

"This is not a laughing matter," the Family Advocate representative spat.His forehead scrunched and his face turned pink.

"Is there any proof of this alleged drugging and what not?" Hana asked.

The other representatives went rigid in their seats with admonishment.

"The father happened to see the needle being stuck in as he lost consciousness."

"So," Hana said slowly. "You want to take the word of a man who not only imprisoned his twelve-year-old son but broke multiple bones in his body as well?

They all frowned with acknowledgement. Condemning his organization was one thing. Not calling out the people who were committing crimes against Bi-Genetics was another.

"We're not saying we agree with what the parents had done. Your people didn't even give us a chance to try and remedy the situation." The Child Welfare representative chided.

"Let me guess. Family counseling, a short stay in foster care before sending him right back into that house, or maybe you'd just do a monthly check in?"

The Health and Human Services representative slammed his fist on the table.

"We are not monsters! We are doing what we can!"

"Without falling out of favor in the public eye. It's no secret how many of the population feel about my kind," Hana snapped.

"We need to work together, or this won't get fixed," the Child Welfare representative said.

Hana endured another hour of childish back and forth banter with accusations flying. When everyone was thoroughly fed up with each other, they left one by one. Sighing with relief at the empty room, he tapped his tablet's commlink and opened the messenger. He found the recipient he wanted and typed two words in bold letters with a thumbs-up emoji.

GOOD JOB.

Back in his newly renovated office, Hana tossed the tablet down on the desk and slid into the chair. He let his head fall back while closing his eyes. All he wanted to do right now was not think about anything. To close his mind and be surrounded by a black pool of empty. Being a part of the Shadow Organization started off as a great idea. Now, he had doubts. A swishing sound from the hall made him perk up and lean forward.

Karias stood in the doorway wearing his layers of robes that dragged on the floor. His body took up the entire frame, blocking light from the hall. Those golden eyes always full of malice peered down on him.

"Did your meeting go well?" Karias asked.

Hana cleared the lump in his throat.

"Of course not. Everyone is being stubborn or clueless."

"What did you expect?"

The alien seemed genuinely curious.

"I'm not sure. Maybe some sense of moving forward. A new era of tolerance for a diverse civilization?" Hana frowned at his own words.

The alien burst out laughing, his voice a sonic boom localized within the section. Hana heard things dropping and people yelped in fright from the onslaught. When he was done, Karias once again gazed at him.

"I have studied your kind's history and I see nothing of the sort. Even in the United States, it took over half a century for them to acknowledge their females and those of other ethnic descent. Other countries still did not do so during the time after that."

"Not all of us think that way. It's a few bad apples spoiling the whole bunch."

"Wrong." Karias's word made Hana flinch. "It has always been the opposite."

Hana knew that. All the same, it still hurt.

His proposal to mirror a plan similar to Metropolis's Ortega City was being perused by all the top heads in the organization and the four aliens brought in to help humanity be on equal footing with the enemy.

"Your plan is flawed the same way your race is," the alien continued. "In order for it to succeed, humans would need to change how their minds work entirely."

"Then what do you suggest?" Hana asked heatedly.

Karias only scoffed and turned to leave.

"Focus on survival. Maybe after humanity is nearly destroyed, the masses will understand."

As he made his way down the hall towards the training entrance, people hugged the walls to give him a wide enough girth. His head almost touched the ceiling.

Hana waited until the alien cleared the corridor and relaxed back in his chair. The picture slideshow on his desk showed various ones of his family. It seemed like only a short time ago that he had been tethered to Professor Makoto. A sting filled his head.

When he no longer needed the old man's affection or approval, a sense of animosity towards him spawned. The Professor treated Hana like a disloyal servant, a spoiled child, and sometimes lashed out at him in anger. Even the first General Perrara fell into the same way of thinking, calling him ungrateful after all the Professor had done for him. Hana had firsthand knowledge of how Professor Makoto operated. Those feelings of guilt for running his facility the way he did weren't sincere.

A knock on the door frame made him look up to see his husband, Scott, leaning against it.

"Lost in thought?"

Hana dropped his head in his hands, covering his face. The tears came so suddenly that it shocked him into gasping. Scott came in and folded his arms around him.

"It's going to be okay. Maybe not now, but in the end. You'll see."

"I'm trying the best I can," Hana cried.

Those arms got tighter, and Hana melted into them. He wasn't trying to change the entire world on his own. He merely wanted to inject the catalyst for it.

THE GRID COMMUNITIES

General Rubio Perrara didn't like it. The Homeland security officers within the organization liked it even less. Despite their misgivings, something had to be done regarding the four inner cities in one state. Since the boom of Bi-Genetics, so much atrocity had occurred and there were always areas where it was worse. The United States was especially egregious considering how much they berated the inflexibility of the more conservative countries. After four days of heated deliberation, a decision was made.

"So, we are all on the same page about this new grid system?" He asked, exploring the faces of his colleagues and guests.

"We should make sure these areas are contained and no one from outside knows what's going on," the Shadowman recruiter, Neil Shannon, said. He was tall with bright red hair and green eyes that seemed to look through, instead of at, you. A killer.

"These communities will be blocked off and upgraded with the newest technology. Our own future city to experiment and see how well we adapt," the assistant to the head of defense added.

"The question becomes, how do we move out the people we don't need and move in the ones we do," another military officer added.

"I have that covered. No reason to do something so drastic. We can offer incentives," Shannon replied.

"Yes, because everyone has a price no matter what they say," a military commander quipped.

Like his father before him, General Perrara stopped for a moment to contemplate the situation. There would be some resistance to the upgrade considering the war may end humanity as they knew it. On the other hand, it would be a last hoorah to show that humans can indeed evolve. When the Shadow Organization began, he had already seen before his father did, signs of the times. The Bi-Genetic population was gearing towards the forty-percentile line and climbing. Regular humans would soon be a minority.

"What's the timeline for monitoring and collecting data?" He asked the recruiter.

"I say about five years. That gives them time to settle into a new environment."

"The range?" The military commander asked.

"Since the cities are in a cluster, we can easily surround them without causing any major reconfiguration of the borders."

"And, there has to be enough amenities within the grids to justify not going outside of it." The Defense Secretary's assistant said.

"Good point," Perrara answered.

He still didn't like it. Too many variables when it came to the population itself. A contingency plan was required in case the whole thing fell apart. The first stage purge would begin and hopefully another wouldn't be necessary. He needed insurance and one name came to mind; Professor Bartley.

〜

Neil Shannon left the meeting with a ton of scenarios swirling in his mind. He had been called in to participate because his expertise was routed in making people disappear. Many of his students worked for various agencies doing just that.

A Grid Community. Interesting.

Its shape and dimensions formed as he walked to his office. The tablet tucked under his arm made a bleep to alert him to a new file. He already knew what it was. While the meeting was still in progress, he requested a profile for every person within those cities. This project would be massive yet stealthy in its inception. With a swipe of his keycard, the door of his office opened. He smirked at the card as he let it zip back up onto the clip. An outdated security measure that was still useful. No one had ever dared to infiltrate the desert location in all the years he'd been there and even if they did, a world of hurt awaited them.

At his desk, he sat down in the plush ergo leather chair and snapped the tablet into the slot on the flat silicon keyboard. He opened the file blinking at him and reared back at the number of profiles being downloaded. The counter kept going for what seemed like eternity until it finally went green and gave a giant check mark.

For all four cities, the population was near the threshold of three million. Daunting, but not impossible. Only half were necessary. He pulled up a hologram map by touching the virtual icon on his desk, zeroing in on the sector. It formed a nice blob with nothing for at least twenty miles on all sides. Perfect. He tapped the mail icon and opened a new message to the military commander in charge of the organization's engineering corp. When he was done, his attention went back to the population file.

His suit jacket stretched tight as he leaned forward, making him conscious of still wearing it. Taking it off, he threw it on the floor, then unbuttoned his shirt to expose the black skintight tunic beneath and rolled up the sleeves.

"This is going to be fun."

He grinned, sitting back with arms crossed.

⌇

Years after the Lancaster incident left a slew of dead bodies and an entire nation in shock, Facility Three was back in full swing. Dr. Lancaster had bioengineered horrific creatures that he unleashed into other facilities via the transport systems. The attacks ended in Lancaster's death and even more frightening revelations to his work. New security measures had been put in place for all the facilities, demanding anyone outside of its boundaries be subject to intense scrutiny.

General Perrara didn't blame Professor Bartley one bit. If he could have predicted the catastrophe ahead of time, he would have found a way to stop Lancaster's madness. He waited for the full body scan to finish and hearing the ding, stepped out into the pure white environment. It always made his father feel disoriented. He found it an advantage, able to see an enemy from any direction.

"This way, please," a tall security guard in a white uniform spoke.

The two men walked in silence, the only sound being their shoes echoing as they struck the tiled floor. In dress blues, Perrara stood out like a moving target. He instinctively smoothed the hair on the edges of his temple and readjusted the cap under his arm. At the end of the corridor a doorway appeared. Inside, the area was muted in color, almost beige.

That's a change.

They walked for ten minutes before stopping at a double door on the right. The guard pressed the commlink.

"General Perrara has arrived."

The doors clicked open, sliding to each side, and the guard gesture with a raised hand for him to enter. General Perrara stepped into a very modern contemporary room with a large conference table. Everything was monochrome in shades of grey, black and white. At the helm was Professor Bartley, barefoot, sitting in a space egg chair. He sat up and extended an arm to the seat next to him.

"General Perrara, good to see you again."

"Likewise." He looked around a bit. "Different setup you got here."

"It's more inviting, I suppose."

"Yes, it is," Perrara sighed as he sat, removing his cap and setting it on the table. "No panel of scientists to negotiate with?"

"Not this time." Professor Bartley's gaze turned dark. "Why have you come here?"

"That's not necessary," Perrara said as he reared back.

"I'm sorry you feel that way but last time there was a secret request, your father got me involved in creating the Shadow Organization."

Perrara winced. True. Still, no reason to be hostile.

"I understand. But you know, I am not my father."

Professor Bartley lowered his eyes and his expression softened.

"I'm sorry. I do know. So, what harbinger of doom have you brought?"

"Nothing so sinister. It does however have a slight quirk that may need a remedy if unsuccessful."

"Smart. What is it?"

"A grid community in four cities of a certain state."

"Come again?"

"We want to create something like your facility except on a larger scale. Each city will be a sector monitored for data collection."

"Ugh," Professor Bartley covered his face with one hand and laid the other on the table. "I don't like that."

"Neither do we, but there has to be a way to gauge how humans fare in advanced situations. We keep growing tech wise. What about the impact on regular people?"

"Another social experiment."

"If you want to categorize it that way, yes. We're going to contain it, but there is no way we can restrict people from leaving it. The threat of comingling is medium."

"Of course it is," Professor Bartley snapped. "You can implant your ideal population all you want, but they are still human. And that is the main problem!"

"Which is why I want you as a fall back," Perrara snapped back.

Both men sat staring at each other in heated anger. Professor Bartley settled into his chair and let out a loud sigh.

"What will this plan be, then?"

"If it all goes to hell, we purge it and your facility takes control."

"Of the territory?"

"Of the government department responsible for Bi-Genetic rights and intake."

Bartley leaned forward, his eyes wide.

"What?"

"It would be apparent that no government can sufficiently protect and serve the Bi-Genetics of this world. The facilities are better equipped to do it. And since you are the head of the facilities..." General Perrara left it at that.

That dark stare returned, and Professor Bartley stood.

He placed both hands on the table and searched the General's face.

"You would have power relinquished to me?"

"Only if it fails. At which point a code will be administered to trigger the event."

"Do you really want to trust me?" Professor Bartley gave a sinister grin.

"Better you than us. Yes." He said it with every bit of conviction he could muster.

"Then I wish you luck." Professor Bartley eased back down in his seat.

"You meant that?" Perrara asked, half-jokingly.

"No." Bartley cocked his head to one side. "I would love nothing better than to strip this world's government of access and control of Bi-Genetics. But I also want to give you all the benefit of the doubt. Prove me wrong."

General Perrara stood up, grabbing his cap.

"We will." He turned to leave at the door said, "It really is nice to see you doing well."

Outside, he was met by a different guard and escorted back the way he had come.

I hope we can prove you wrong, Professor. But my faith is wavering too.

~

The two Shadow organization spies met at a busy restaurant on the far end of one of the cities to discuss their plans. Zach Reimer worked for the Secretary of Interior and Stan Maples was a project manager for the Fair Housing Committee. They figured personally getting a lay of the land would benefit their agenda. The place was on a higher scale above family dining and overly priced.

Reimer scanned the menu with a deep frown. His hair was slicked back neat and tight, speckles of gray at the temples and his wire rimmed glasses were the latest fashion. With well-manicured fingers, he held the booklet as if it was going to attack him. The tailored suit fit him snugly, showing that he did indeed workout.

Across from him, Stan perused his menu with no real emotion. He was overworked and tired. His suit, a department store special trying its best to make him look the part of government important, was already crinkled. His hair's meticulous grooming had long come undone from scratching it in frustration most of the day.

"How can a Caesar Salad cost sixteen dollars?" Reimer said in irritation as he let the menu drop from his hands. It made a loud snap on the glass table. "Is Caesar himself coming to make the damn thing?"

"Let's not make a scene over a salad," Stan pleaded. "We're not here for the food anyway." His stomach contested. "Though I should probably eat something."

"Whatever." Reimer snapped his fingers at the nearby server. "You, we need to order."

Stan winced as he watched the server's face scrunch up while pivoting towards them. He took a sip of his ice water and waited for the inevitable terse exchange.

"I am not your server, sir," the young man said. "I'll let them know you are ready."

Before the man could turn away, Reimer blurted out, "Do you work here or not?"

"Sir," the young man began to reply and was cut off.

"We are busy men. On a time limit. Now, we want two Tuscan chickens. No fucking tomatoes! With Caesar salads on the side. Two ice teas, unsweetened. Go tell our server and get the order in. Thank you."

Reimer handed both menus to the server who reluctantly took them and headed towards the order station. Stan kept his head down the whole time, not wanting to engage. Being an operative didn't mean he liked drawing attention to himself. Especially on an assignment.

"Did you really?" He asked.

"Hmph! Maybe that little shit will work for a change. Seems like a spoiled underachiever. Why else would he be working in this place?"

He had to agree on that. It still irked him every time his counterpart was so abrasive.

"Can we just talk about how this area needs to be reconfigured.?"

"Oh, it will definitely need an overhaul. This," he circled the air above him with one finger, "is one of the first things to go. Put in a real Italian joint. High class."

"We need to keep some semblance of it. A lot of middle class people actually come to these types of eateries for networking and gossip."

Reimer let out a deep breath. He grabbed his water and gulped down half of it.

"So, what do you think?"

"More houses than high rises. Keep it more residential to induce that community feel we want. Only major businesses and government agencies need taller buildings."

"Are you going to do that with all four sectors?" Reimer raised his eyebrows.

The previous server came with the ice teas and set the glasses down hard enough to make the sound peak interest from other patrons. Lips pursed, the server looked downward at them before walking away. A lemon that had seen fresher days set at the top of each drink.

"I didn't ask for lemon!" Reimer called after him while he fished them out and tossed both on the table's edge.

"It's fine," Stan said.

"No, it's not. You always do that. Stop letting people walk over you, even if it's a mission. Anyway," he took a sip of the iced tea and made a face. "God, that's awful! How about we do a mirror effect?"

"You mean all four sectors, built cookie cutter?"

"Mm hmm," he nodded. "That way we know where everything is located regardless of which one we're looking at."

"That would cut down costs, buy in bulk."

"See? You thought I couldn't help you as much."

He gave an arrogant wink only he could pull off.

A different server came with a steaming plate on each arm with two small salads. She gave a wide smile.

"Two Tuscan chickens?"

"Right here, darling." Reimer patted the table and she set them down.

"So sorry about the confusion. I had to take over an extra section."

"Don't let them work you to death in here."

"No sir. I make sure that doesn't happen." She stood straight, hands clasped together in front of her. "Enjoy your lunch." Again, with the big smile.

"I like you," Reimer said, his fork pointed at her. She walked away, and he turned back to Stan. "That's how you do customer service."

"Right."

Stan lifted his fork and cut a piece of chicken off.

"We got a plan down, then?"

The chicken was already halfway into his mouth. Deciding to commit to his hunger, he bit down and chewed before answering.

"Yes, we have a plan."

"Good," Reimer said with a mouth full of food. "We can go over the details later."

I hate working with this guy.

Even so, he knew Reimer was a beast when it came to getting shit done. The high price to pay for efficiency.

They toiled on the project for weeks, crunching numbers and setting up contacts. At the next meeting, a large schematic was displayed on the holoscreen for everyone in the conference room to scrutinize. The joint effort of Reimer, Stan, and the recruiter were paying off. General Perrara wanted to clap his hands in praise, except it was premature. The real test would be when the grid was fully implemented. It was his off day, so he wore a light colored casual suit with a crew neck shirt and spit shined loafers. Compared to the other three, he looked like a man ready to vacation on a yacht. Not being on duty didn't mean he had to be sloppy. He never understood how people could just roll out of bed and put on anything.

"Gentlemen, this is a great endeavor. The progress you've made is remarkable."

Stan, in dress shirt and jeans, scratched his head and grinned.

"Believe me, it was not easy task. But thanks to Reimer, we nailed it down under budget and ahead of the timeline."

"And on your end?" Perrara asked Neil.

"Tying up some loose ends." He said nothing more and the air in the room became tense.

It was no mystery how some of the Bi-Genetics were being acquired. Their families were given the incentives of moving away from judgmental neighbors in exchange for not throwing the children to facilities.

"Make sure we don't raise any red flags along the way."

"It's too late for that!" Reimer snorted.

They all looked up at the holoscreen. A massive area turned into a confined fortress comprised of four small cities with the center making up a smaller fifth. Each section was assigned a number and within those were codes for every household and business.

Like lab rats in a cage ready for processing.

〜

Agent X sat in his sedan parked across from one of the prestigious neighborhood's three-story homes. Lots of high end vehicles in the driveways along with sculpted lawns. All a ruse to hide what kind of people lived there. Not quite rich, they were affluent and nasty to those not of the same status. Let alone their hatred for evolved humans which he found comical since so many vied for the chance to have their DNA altered for longevity.

Birds chirped in the trees and a light breeze ruffled his hair through the half-opened windows. A nice day for a shake down. He waited for the expensive SUV to pull into the driveway and the occupants filed out. Immediately, he witnessed the abuse of the middle child. At fourteen, the boy was fairly tall for his age and prettier than most. His hand slipped as he tried to wrestle a grocery bag from the trunk and his mother was on him lightning fast, slamming his head against the side of the hatch.

"Be careful! If anything gets crushed, you don't eat tonight. Got it?"

"Sorry," the kid mumbled, still disoriented.

Blood trickled from his forehead.

His siblings paid no heed, except for the oldest who smirked and continued into the house. The father glanced up and saw the blood.

"Shit, Dana! You caused a cut!"

He grabbed the bag from the boy's arms and used his foot to push him towards the house.

"Go clean that shit up!"

The mother seethed with anger at her own actions as she took him by the arm and yanked him in. From his vantage point in the car, Agent X found the bathroom window and watched her roughly treat his wound. Nearby neighbors had also been watching and the disdain on their faces told him plenty. That boy would disappear soon if he didn't act fast.

Only a week before, three of the neighbor boys ambushed him on the side of a convenience store. He didn't interfere at first because the kid getting an ass kicking was nothing new. But when the boys had him on the ground and he heard what they were saying, he did sort of panic. Which was unusual for a veteran spy like himself.

"I heard they like it when you beat the shit out of them," the first boy had said.

"Yeah, they shift so you can do 'em," the second added.

"That true?" The last boy asked him. "You like that shit?"

The kid got visibly scared and started shaking his head.

"Let's all get a piece of that ass," the second said. "Who wants first dibs?"

They beat him with punches and kicks until he did shift. The store owner had come out to intervene earlier but when the kid shifted, he frowned in disgust and went back inside. Bloody and helpless, the kid still tried to get away. Two of the boys held the kid down while the other pulled his pants off then pulled his own down.

He was mere inches from violating the kid when Agent X threw an empty beer bottle that way. Shards sprayed on the exposed boy's midriff as it shattered against the wall above. The boys cried out in surprise and jumped away from the kid. Suddenly afraid to be witnessed, they hurried off, the one boy shaking glass from his crotch as he rounded the corner. That was the day Agent X decided to up his mission's timeline.

In the passenger seat was an envelope with brochures and legal documents along with a live check. Those were rare and only issued by the banks for big amounts that could be verified. So far, it left a favorable impression on the candidates. He saw the front door shut after the last of the groceries were hauled in. Grabbing the package, he got out of his car and walked up the driveway. There was the sound of people bustling inside as he neared the door and he thought with that much money, the house should have been soundproofed. Shoulders squared, Agent X rang the doorbell. Not even three seconds went by before the door flew open. The mother stood in the frame staring at him with anger.

"We don't take solicitors! Read the damn sign!"

She had a hand on the door ready to slam it when he produced his fake Health and Child Services credentials.

"Not a solicitor, ma'am."

Her face drained of color and she nervously looked back into the house.

"Umm, we just got back from the store and the house is not…don't you schedule house visits first?" There was a tinge of her anger returning. Inwardly, he scoffed at the woman's sudden attempt to being polite and acting like a civilized adult.

"Impromptu ones, no. May I come in?"

He made sure to convey it wasn't an option.

"Please," she gestured with a slight head bow.

Once inside, he quickly canvased the nearby rooms with his eyes to know where everything was in case an incident occurred. The rest of the family became picture perfect the moment the mother whispered who he was. Her husband went rigid and glanced nervously at the kid loading their produce in the refrigerator's lower compartment, paying them no mind.

"Shall we have a seat to discuss some business?" He asked.

"Yes, yes," the father answered.

The father took his wife by the arm and raised a hand to the sitting room a few yards away.

"The whole family, if you don't mind."

"Oh," the mother said.

They reluctantly motioned for their children to follow. The kid was slow to rise due to his injuries not quite healed and his head probably ringing from the new one. He shut the refrigerator and joined his family. Each member had their own favorite place to sit but the look their mother gave let them know to sit on the sofa, all together, with the kid on the end.

Who buys a giant couch that fits six people? He thought. Cream leather, no less.

The next to the oldest son had his smart phone, raising it up out of reach as his mother leaned over and finally snatched it from him. He looked up ready to say something unpleasant by his expression then stopped as his gaze landed on Agent X. Indignant, he slouched against the sofa, arms folded.

"So," the mother began. "What brings you to our home for a visit?"

"Are you really asking me that?"

Every person's face except the kid's flushed pink. The father shifted in his seat.

"The neighbors, wasn't it? How else would your department know."

"Among other incidents."

The oldest son gave the kid a furious stare that defied reason. Agent X almost reacted to save him if the older brother made a move. There was so much hostility in the air, it nearly suffocated him. The last time he felt something so strong was in enemy territory during his tour in the Middle East way back when. These were Americans and thus far the worst human beings he had seen decrying the treatment of others in different countries.

Hypocrites.

"In light of all this, we understand you wish to find a resolution."

"A resolution?" The mother asked. "I never said anything to anyone about…" She stopped talking and her eyes went wide.

"Gossip is a funny thing but very valuable in these circumstances," Agent X said.

The father frowned. He too had voiced some horrifying ideas regarding his son to many of his colleagues at work.

Agent X set the packet on the table between them.

"There is a new community opening about sixty miles from here. All state of the art homes with every amenity imaginable. Great schools and a crime free environment." The contents were removed one by one. He watched their reaction to the live check. "Of course, there is one contingency, as you will see in the documents."

He waited for them to peruse the information, the oldest son also given them to read. After a few minutes had passed, he tossed the papers onto the table, making them spiral everywhere.

"Gregory!" His mother shouted.

"What? We just move someplace so he can be safe, and we have to adapt to strangers who probably look down on us?"

The father eyed the check, then glanced around and back at the check. He looked down the sofa at the kid who had fallen asleep without anyone noticing. The corner of the man's right eye twitched.

"And that's all we have to do? Make sure he's safe and sound and we get a new life with all this money to do as we please?"

"That's it."

"And if we don't?" The second son retorted.

Agent X gave them a dark stare that made them all shrink back in fear.

"Then the deal is forfeit. An appropriate punishment will be implemented."

The kid's eyes fluttered open.

Relief emanated from them.

⌒

Intake at the new grid city entrances was much like the first days of training for Neil. He manned an office a few blocks from the first entry and watched the influx of data as each family checked in. Moving trucks, portable storage containers and multiple vehicles jammed the four lane roads on all sides. His plan was to move to each entrance periodically to make sure everything went smoothly.

Stan was working on last minute infrastructure issues while Reimer cursed, and berated government officials put in place to oversee the communities. Stan was grateful not having to work with that man at this stage of the project. On the screen to his left were the images from the giant x-rays built into the gated walls. They stood fifty feet and extended the checkpoint by almost thirty so that even a twenty-four-foot truck could be fully scanned.

Two years in the making and he was pleased to an extent. Some of the families slotted to move had forfeit their spots, not being able to restrain themselves from harming their Bi-Genetic child. That depleted his expected soldier count and he didn't like it when his agenda was undermined by selfish regular humans. Earth needed all the fighters it could muster and to this day, many failed to understand the dire consequences in killing off evolved children.

A loud beep interrupted his thoughts and he turned to the scanner image.

"You have got to be joking!" He yelled.

On the screen was a sedan with four occupants and a fifth in the trunk with barely a heat signature. Gate agents rushed to the vehicle and an argument ensued. Neil grabbed his keys and went to his car. He drove faster than the posted speed limit and arrived right as one of the guards laid a hand on his revolver.

"Keep that weapon stowed!" He got out and went up to the driver side of the vehicle. "What is the meaning of this?"

"We have the correct paperwork! Why are we being stopped?" The male driver asked.

"The issue is the body in your damn trunk!"

The man went red.

His wife and children became agitated.

"We brought him, didn't we? There wasn't room in the back seat."

Neil stepped back in awe at the man's audacity. He went through a series of resolutions in his mind while he contemplated killing the man. This was a dilemma. Should he let them in and hope they keep their end of the bargain going forward or turn them away, leading to the death of a valuable child? With clenched fists and teeth, he made a decision.

"Get out of the vehicle," he snapped.

He motioned for the rear guards to open the trunk. One of them stepped up and hit the release button on the steering panel.

"You are being reassigned until we have an all-clear from medical."

The family huddled together and watched the guard gently lift the boy out of the trunk. His limbs flopped loosely, an arm and leg clearly broken. He was wrapped in a sheet with blood stains seeped through. Gasps from people in other vehicles nearby filled the air.

This is why I hate my own kind.

BREAKDOWN OF SOCIETY

And it gets worse with each year, Hoskins Sr. thought to himself.

Looking not a day over fifty since having alien DNA injected into him at the beginning of the alien and human alliance, he sat in exile on an island off the coast of a neutral zone following his escape from the hands of U.S. persecution. They had sealed him up in a metal cell with no way to communicate outside. The guards never spoke to him even when asked a question. His son was surely on a target list by that time and would probably be caught as well. The one who released him was that amazon alien bitch. She had looked down on him as if he were a cockroach. Scared the living shit out of him, made him piss his pants. That's what angered him more than anything. He let her get under his skin and show weakness.

American soldiers don't show fear to nobody.

He wanted to find out her motive for letting him go then thought spending another second in the same breathing area as that monster was a bad idea. Whatever the reason, he was more than grateful. Never the less, something nagged him about the whole thing. Her eyes had a gleam in them that gave you a sense of despair. She was playing a game with human lives as collateral.

When he fled, finding his contacts still in place, his first order of business was to find out about his idiot son.

Sure enough, he found him hiding in the jungle with his second family of half darkies. He wasn't sure which was worse; the half breed alien wife or the uncultured jungle whore. The mistake his son made was not expanding his forces to incorporate world leaders. Guerilla fighters were good for small stuff, but all-out war was nearly upon them.

Hoskins was no fool. As patriotic as he was, he also knew there was no benefit in humans being wiped out over stupid stuff. His attempts to nip the fight in the bud with a new missile long ago were misunderstood.

An article about the rise of those Biodes and the crimes against them was paused on his tablet. He stopped reading it halfway because of the disgust he felt. His animosity towards them didn't mean they weren't useful. Killing them off was just a waste of resources. Add an alien war on top of it all and he shook his head in bewilderment at the governments' lack of oversight. At least when he had a hold of those tainted humans, they fought to keep order.

"Hey boss," a man in dark shades and a suit called out.

Hoskins turned his head to get a better look at who it was. The man was a hired muscle who always got the job done, no matter what it entailed. An all-rounder of crime.

"What's up?"

The man stopped next to him and shoved his hands in his pants pockets. He looked out at the ocean for a brief moment then turned his attention to Hoskins.

"About that Shadow organization that ain't so secret anymore."

Heat rose in Hoskins' face as he remembered the senior General Perrara. Part of his downfall was tied to that bastard, but he calmed himself, forgiving the actions of his former nemesis.

"Yeah, what's going on with it now?"

"Looks like a new project. Saw a whole cluster of cities

bordered off. From the outside, nothing strange but we know otherwise."

Hoskins pulled himself upright in the lounge chair.

"Did you say cities?"

"Four of them."

"What the hell?" He snapped his fingers at the man who then produced a smaller tablet from inside his jacket. An aerial shot was brought up and the cluster was visible. He used his fingers to zoom in and saw how each sector was mirrored to each other. "You sons of bitches!" From that image alone, he knew what they were up to. He also knew it would fail miserably.

Might as well get in on the action

"I want to know all they got in there and how to get in."

"Hate to break it to you, boss, but you kinda' stick out, being famous and all."

"No one gives a damn about me anymore since that dumbass went and ruined everything."

Which was probably not true, yet he decided to test the waters anyway. What were Perrara and his pantywaist agents supposed to do when the one who released him could wipe them out in a heartbeat? A thought came to him. His mouth formed a big old grin.

Flight or fight mode kicked in the moment Erica, Chad Hoskins's ex-wife, opened the door to find her former father in law standing there smiling wide with two thugs behind him scanning the area. Her current husband was working at the hospital and her guns were in the bedroom closet. She forced her heart rate to normalize. There was no escaping the situation. One of her neighbors walked past and waved. She gleefully waved back.

"Why are you here?" She asked him.

He feigned astonishment then snorted.

"Sweetheart, you know better than that. I don't talk business outside." All three men bulldozed their way into the house, the last man shutting the door. "Nice. You got rid of the heavy curtains. More sunlight coming in. You anticipate catching some fleas coming your way?"

She understood the code for enemy intruders and that was exactly right. As a Shadow agent, she had to be more on guard these days. Her husband too.

"Nature of the job," she replied.

In the living room, Hoskins sat down on the love-seat near the windows and leaned back, making himself comfortable. He stretched his legs out under the glass table.

"Got anything to drink around here? Mighty hot out and Southern hospitality is key here."

She pursed her lips and gave him an angry stare.

"Them too?" She pointed to his two companions.

"Absolutely!" He nodded to them. "Feeling parched?"

"I could use something cold to drink," his right-hand man said while the other nodded.

"Don't move," she ordered.

She walked into the kitchen and did her best to stop her hands from shaking as she set up a drink tray with four glasses. The half full pitcher of strawberry lemonade was sitting on the top shelf in the refrigerator for easy access. Placed on the tray, she maneuvered it to the middle and carried it out.

"Well look at that," Hoskins cried out. "Fancy even."

The other men sat down, one on the other side of the loveseat, the other in the matching chair on the end of the table. When she was done pouring and distributing, she sat down on the couch across from Hoskins and waited. They sipped their drinks.

"Whew! That hits the spot."

Hoskins smacked his lips.

She opened her mouth to say something, raising from her seat.

"Ah ah," Hoskins chided. "No going for your weapons." She sat back down. "This is just a friendly family visit."

"Family?" She hissed the word through her teeth.

"Oh, come on, we both know you could have snapped my son's neck at any time. Of course, if you had, I'd have killed you my damn self. An ass he may be, but he's still my son."

This time she stood fully, ready to take them on in hand to hand combat to get them out of her home. Her ex-husband nearly killed her, and this jackass wants to come in and threaten her? *Fuck that!* She took off her thin sweater and tossed it behind onto the couch. The two men stopped midway sipping their drinks and looked towards Hoskins.

He let out a long sigh and waved a hand at her to sit back down.

"Now, I'm not saying I condone how he treated you. His momma didn't raise him that way. I sure as shit never hit my wife. No idea where he got that from." Hoskins shamefully shook his head. "Sit back down. We ain't fighting today."

She reluctantly did as he asked.

"So, what? Why now? You hate Bi-Genetics and I'm one."

"Ah, but you got my grandkids. That's a little different. And I don't hate your kind. Just think you all would be much more useful as tools instead of regular old citizens."

"And you want to use me as one of your tools?" She snapped.

"That's right. You see, your screwed-up organization is looking to remedy their flaws, but it will make things harder for you. Don't you want to help out your fellow freaks?" He eyed her viciously while swirling his glass.

"What the hell are you talking about?" She growled in frustration.

The way he smiled let her know she was in the dark on something very important, putting her at a disadvantage. She glanced quickly at the small table holding a large vase where a gun was stashed inside. If it came to that, she had a chance. Hoskins drank some more of his lemonade. Once again, the Shadow Organization had put her in a bad situation.

⌒

Never, in all his years as an agent, had Kevin been so surprised. After the whole debacle with Hoskins Jr., the exit of Professor Makoto and a chain of command collapse in the organization, he decided to go rogue. No one stopped or questioned him. This of course meant he was able to dive deeper into what made it tick. That was his first mission from Professor Morandi decades ago. That was quickly abandoned. He wasn't doing this for her anymore. She made it clear how much she cared about him when a team of her personal soldiers came knocking. He killed every last one and sent their livers, specially packed, back to her. She went into hiding soon after.

From his spot atop a hill overlooking the valley, he sat on the grass wearing optical enhancer contact lenses. He let them adjust the zoom until the details of the cities were crystal clear. A breeze came through and he pulled his long-sleeved flak jacket closed. The camouflage pants were unnecessary, just worn for comfort. His black tank top hugged him, showing the definition of his abdomen. A year and a half of hair growth had his sandy brown hair hitting the tops of his shoulders. His daughter liked it better that way.

This is like something out of a Sci-Fi script. He thought, concerning the view.

He couldn't fathom how the higher ups thought no one would notice the difference in structure, let alone the set up. The tallest building was no more than fifteen floors, but the architecture was so far advanced that it almost reminded him of Metropolis; the failed experiment his former counterpart created and to this day was still trying to perfect. Humans really weren't ready.

A soft klaxon sounded from his satchel and he fished out the commlink.

"Kevin." There was a pause on the other end. "You got two seconds," he warned.

"Wasn't sure you would actually pick up," the voice on the other said.

"I did. What are you after?"

"Don't go near that place."

"Not even going to give it the benefit of the doubt?" Kevin laughed.

"Are you?"

"Hell no. But I want to see it up close and personal."

"There's no way to get in without Hana or that creepy ass recruiter finding out."

"Oh?" Kevin made a playful expression.

"What will you do in there? Watch it crumble and do nothing?"

Kevin contemplated that for a bit. Would he? No. He also wouldn't interfere no matter how bad until there was a clear resolution.

"I'm going in."

"Then all I can say is be careful and don't get caught."

The line went dead, and he shoved the commlink back into his bag.

Yep, this was not a good idea. His kids would be excited though. Living in a bunker for so long takes a toll and they would happily trade it for a nice neighborhood in a city with tons of stuff to do. His lenses readjusted and landed on the building right smack in the middle of all four sectors. A giant monolith communication relay masquerading as an art structure.

"That's my ticket in," he murmured to himself.

For the umpteenth time, someone was hacking into the main grid's system and trying to access information. Neil knew it was bound to happen, but the number of attempts was staggering. Some were caught and traced back to the culprits. Nosy government shits wanting to see what was going on inside the cities. Others were hackers looking for a challenge. Then there were the ones doing strange things like fixing data or getting in only to back out. Like they were testing its integrity.

A small team of grid monitors watched the influx from within the main buildings positioned on the outskirts of each city. Next to each one was a police department and a government agency. So far neither of those were getting hacked. His gut, unable to pinpoint the source, told him something was amiss. There was a sick feeling he couldn't shake. It was too early in the game to purge the whole thing and start over.

He stood in front of massive holoscreens that circled above him. Twenty in all, they spanned upwards inside the monolith. Everything seemed fine. Nice neighborhoods where the people looked out for each other; on the surface. There lay the problem. He felt a headache coming on.

The craziest thought hit Kevin as he helped unload the moving truck sitting in his new driveway. Not six houses down from him another person was moving in and the moment Hoskins Sr. got out of the car, Kevin froze. When would an opportunity to take out that sack of shit ever come along again? Something stopped him from dropping the box in his hand and going in the house for his gun. No. He decided to do the unthinkable. The chance of Hoskins possibly knowing him was a non-issue.

With a big smile and a strong wide gait, he strolled over to the former General looking ridiculous in casual clothes. Kevin marked the button-down shirt as department store and the cargo pants from a high-end store. He too was wearing something similar that fit him way better. Hoskins had acquired a small gut, so the pants didn't quite sit well on his waist. The straw fedora with wide black band completed the ensemble, making him appear a tourist.

"Good afternoon!" Kevin called out to him.

He raised an arm to wave, sure to let the man standing next to Hoskins see his well-toned muscles. In a white 'wife beater' tank and opened short sleeved shirt he probably reminded people of a thug. His long hair didn't help any.

Hoskins turned to him and instant recognition showed in his eyes. He smiled and walked over to meet him halfway.

"Well, ain't this a kick in the ass," Hoskins laughed.

"Hmm. I almost took you out."

"And, why didn't you?"

Hoskins glanced back at his two goons.

"Because this would be much more fun."

"I think I'm gonna' agree with you on that."

He looked around the neighborhood.

"Come to see the demise first hand?"

"Unlike you, I will find a remedy before it goes down in flames," Kevin retorted.

"Like me? Son, I don't want this shit going to pot any more than you do."

"Then why are you here?"

"No need in your Shadow group having all the fun."

"Not my group." Kevin shrugged.

"Oh, ho! Jumped the nest? Good for you."

A young man wearing a US Navy PT uniform came out of the house. His dark hair was in a crew cut and the body muscles rippled as he walked. Kevin raised an eyebrow at Hoskins.

"My oldest grandson. Piece of work, ain't he?"

Kevin watched the young man grab some more boxes and head back in. He could make out some of his mother's features, though, mostly Hoskins'.

"Just you and him?"

"Nah, he got some woman he met while on shore leave. I'm an old man who needs to be looked after, ya' know?"

"Yeah, that alien DNA really isn't working."

The two of them stood staring at each other until the sound of a trunk slamming broke the mood. A woman across the street hefted up a grocery bag and nodded at them. They both waved.

"You should come down for dinner soon," Hoskins said, not taking his eyes off the woman.

"Same to you," Kevin replied, also watching her.

"Damn spies," they said in unison as they looked back at each other.

Agent X pulled his sunglasses down halfway to get a better look at the scene happening a block down from his sector. The heads decided he would be more valuable inside the community, so he abandoned his personal hideout for a nice house in the suburbs. Wearing casual clothes and flip flops, he sat on his porch drinking a glass of scotch. He often did that in the early evening because things happened around then. With all the extractions he had completed, it was a no brainer that the project may fail. Oh, there was heaps of hope, though reality was biting them in ass.

Well that didn't take long.

Two grown men took down a teenage boy in broad daylight and began kicking him. A few yards away was another boy being held back a woman, presumably his mother. Nearby neighbors went into action to stop them, admonishing the two men while they all looked around in a panic. He heard the whoop of sirens getting closer. The boy was helped up and dragged into one of the neighbor's house as law enforcement came driving up next to the sidewalk.

In only two years, the people had reverted to their hatred of Bi-Genetics though Agent X had to admit, not to the full extent like previously. Incentives only went so far. Telling parents with murderous intent who refuse to understand their own child to be nice and learn more was a waste of energy. There were a few converts. The head recruiter was found pulling his hair out on a daily basis. Agent X stopped going to check on the man for fear of witnessing a meltdown.

Both officers exited the patrol car and scanned the area. All parties had fled the scene, so they would have to knock on doors and ask for a report. If no one was willing to explain, the officers were to contact the main hub to see street footage. It behooved the residents to fess up and tell what happened. One of the officers caught his eye and they nodded at each other.

His commlink tinged in his ear and he tapped it.

"What do you think?" The male voice asked.

"It's a riot to watch, that's for sure."

"I don't really find it funny."

"Because you have a giant rod up your ass. Situation is under control. The kid wasn't hurt that bad."

"That's not the issue." A deadly silence followed.

Agent X rolled his eyes and let out a loud sigh.

"If it looked like it was getting out of hand, I would have intervened. These people aren't stupid. Neighbors did their job."

"I hope these incidents level out and we can work on advancements in the next few years."

"Sure."

The commlink went silent and Agent X leaned back to watch the officers knock on the first door.

Good luck with that dream.

UNDERWORLD TRADE

Each sector had been appointed a community leader to oversee progress, report information and transmit updates from the main hub. With crime on the rise, a secret meeting was called for a resolution. Since the communities were their responsibility, they felt no need to let the architects or higher ups in on it.

The police Chief, and leader of Sector One, got his colleagues attention. A small conference room with soundproof walls was created inside the third leader's home. They had a hard time getting the materials for the walls before Hoskins helped smuggle them in. As far as they knew, he was merely an old military man with connections, nothing more.

"We must figure this thing out sooner than later, gentlemen." He nodded to the fourth leader, "and Lady Mayor. Things are dire."

"That is an understatement," the City Attorney who lead the third sector said.

"Look, there is no way these Bi-Genetics are going to get any better treatment. You can't change a person's stripes that quick." The planning director in charge of Sector Two added.

"I am not a fan of them but I'm no monster like some of these parents," the mayor said.

The Director leaned forward on the table.

"How about we make it okay only in certain settings?"

The rest of the leaders went quiet and stared at him in shocked indignation.

"Oh, come off it!" He yelled. "We all know that's the answer. All they want to do is act out their frustration about Bi-Genetics ON Bi-Genetics."

"As painful as it is, that's true," the police chief replied.

"So, what, a pain room?" The Mayor asked.

"Some ungodly sex trade?" The city attorney threw out.

The Director's face changed, and he didn't speak for a long time.

"That might work," he finally said.

"What?" The other leaders asked together.

"Both. And maybe something else, too."

"God help us," the police chief whispered.

"We're about to be annihilated by aliens! God went out of the equation a long time ago," the Director retorted.

⸺

Midnight was a few minutes away yet the streets outside of a newly opened nightclub was buzzing with activity on a weekday. Attendants held open the doors of high end vehicles to let well-dressed people climb out. Bass heavy techno music blasted from the club guarded by tall men in black suits. Laser lights danced across the sky in vibrant colors.

Inside was a blast of lights, confetti, music and alcohol. The din of voices layered with the thump of speakers straining against the onslaught of beats. On either side of the club sat a full bar glowing with neon borders so patrons knew where to refuel. Beyond the stage where the DJ stood immersed in his craft was a long corridor painted black. Small LED lights lined the ceiling giving it an eerie ambience. The music became muted immediately at the entrance and stayed that way all the way to the end.

A door painted red had a sign in scripted font.

Members Only.

A couple held their wrists to the electronic reader on the door and it clicked open. The room on the other side was dimly lit but they could make out four round red cushions occupied by other couples. A closer look at one of them, they saw an older man groping a young man who appeared to be out of it. Even so, the young man was attempting to get away with no success. The older man finally got him down and pulled off his pants. He had already taken his own down around his knees.

Further in, was an archway and heightened voices could be heard. Arriving, the couple found a room full of people. There were at least twelve adults in various forms of sitting and standing around a large cushion in the middle. Three men were atop what appeared to be a young girl that couldn't be any older than fourteen. One of the men finished his turn and moved away for the next man to start. The third was holding her arms down. His skin, flushed pink from exertion, indicated he must have been the first. She was clearly drugged, but tears streaked her face. Bruises were forming on her wrists and thighs, the men being none too gentle as they thrust into her like animals.

A server in a white shirt and black vest came up to the couple, offering a pre-made cocktail. The woman mouthed thank you, while taking one. Her husband was stiff next to her and when she looked up frowned. Horrified, he was completely still. His eyes were wide open, nearly bulging out of their sockets. He turned to leave, and she grabbed his arm.

"Don't you dare, leave me in here," she seethed.

"What the fuck?" he whispered angrily.

"What? She's one of those Biodes. Who cares?"

"That's someone's child!" His fingers dug into his clenched hands.

"Obviously the parents don't care."

"Is that what you'd do with our son?"

The woman stopped midway into sipping her drink. Her hands shook a little.

"Of course not!" She snapped. "That's what the facilities are for. I'm not a monster!"

That was not what he wanted to hear. Clamping a hand over his mouth, he made a beeline for the restrooms. His wife raised her glass again and heard the man on the girl let out a loud grunt, signaling his turn was over. She tossed the whole content of the drink down her throat and went after her husband. A quick glance around the room found the viewers engrossed with the scene. Some were agitated, a few sexually excited and the others made her cringe. They had no reaction to it at all. Like it was the most normal thing to see.

The reason she had become a member was to indulge herself and sometimes let her husband watch. Her status as a community liaison made her eligible. When she heard what the membership entailed, she jumped at the chance to see if the rumors about Bi-Genetics were true. It was no secret, many of the residence had ill will towards them. Seeing something like this was a bit shocking. This was the first time she had been to this club and thinking she wouldn't be back.

A man in a long black robe came out from the side door next to the cushion and waved the men off. They lumbered over the edge and gathered their clothes from the floor.

"That is the end of this session."

There were a few grumbles.

"The next one will be in thirty minutes with a fresh specimen." Sighs of relief.

Yes, you can all get your turn tonight.

He went over to the girl and scrutinized the bruises.

Barbarians.

Lifting her with gentle ease, he carried her back through the side door. Four hospital beds lined the wall equipped with their own sinks and I.V. drips if necessary. He placed her on one then went to the sink and wet a towel. There was a sprayer, but he felt it may cause more pain. While he wiped the human muck from her skin, his assistant burst in followed by the girl's father.

"He got here early and demanded to come retrieve his child."

The father was red faced and out of breath. His stare landed on the bruises and he went a shade darker.

"What the fuck?" He yelled. "We have family coming over in the morning! How are we supposed to explain that kind of damage?"

"Shut up," the man ordered. "You brought your child here for these people to do whatever they wanted in exchange for status and money. You don't get to be angry."

The father merely sputtered, not saying another word.

The man continued to wipe her entire body until he was satisfied. He picked up a slimline injection gun and a vial of clear liquid from the side of the sink. It was inserted into the syringe gun's slot and carefully injected each bruise. Within minutes, they disappeared, and her skin was pristine again. Removing the first vial, he loaded a second filled with orange liquid. He used his fingers to locate the pressure point on her side and injected slowly.

She convulsed violently as her body began to shift back to its original male form. All the while, cut off screams emitted from their mouth due to the previous

47

drug preventing full use of the vocal chords.

"Shh, everything is okay."

The man stroked the now young boy's hair at the same time he snapped his fingers at his assistant. Another syringe was placed in his hand and he gave the boy a sedative. Once he was still and fast asleep, the man turned to his father.

"You can take him now."

"Where are his damn clothes?" The father demanded, looking around frantically.

The assistant handed him a bag.

"In there. You can just wrap him up in this sheet and be on your way."

"Now, you look here," the father began.

The man was on him in a flash, so close they shared breath.

"Take your child and go," he said slowly.

Frightened, the father threw the bag across his shoulder, tossed the sheet around his son, and ran out. The assistant stood next to him.

"I'm not going to lie, boss. This shit is totally fucked up."

"Yes, it is."

"I guess, at least we heal them before sending them home."

"Their subconscious will never be healed."

"I meant physically," the assistant replied.

"I know what you meant. That doesn't make it go away. And until someone stops it, things may get worse. It's only been a little over a year."

"Who can stop it? The goddamn sector leaders are running this shit!"

"Exactly."

The man cleaned up the station and went through a different door on the other side.

Time to get the next one ready for the greedy masses.

Hoskins walked out of a nightclub in another sector, his two thugs in tow, while he cleaned his teeth with a plastic pick. The food was marginal in his opinion and the dress code was a farce. He didn't need to dress to the nines for a place filled with uppity shitheads waiting for a chance to get their hands on a Biode. A truly disgusting turn of events in the five years since it started.

Knowing the project would fail he never expected a full blown downward spiral into debauchery. The rumors kept spiraling, yet he never felt the desire to see for himself. That changed when his youngest grandson had come to visit, and a community liaison approached him. He told the jackass he'd think about it then contacted a hacker to make sure he was on the members list.

"What do you think, Hoss?" His right-hand man asked.

"Shameful. I made sure my Terrors never had sexual contact with each other."

"You did have them on pretty strong birth control too," his second man added.

"Damn right." The attendant pulled up with their vehicle and hopped out, tossing the keys to his right-hand man. "Let's get the hell out of here!"

The second held up a small device to the attendant's wrist until it bleeped. A blue bar running across the bottom turned green with the words transfer complete.

"Thank you, sir." The attendant was off again to get the next car.

During the ride home, Hoskins sat in silence. The turn of events jarred him. He was always adamant about his feelings towards those Bi-odes and the aliens being here to begin with. His tactic was to get all the data on how much of a weapon they could be used as and thought of nothing else. Now he understood what the other world leaders and scientists were hinting at. He never paid it any mind because it was such a trivial issue in light of the war.

Disappointment in humanity fell on him like a ton of bricks. All his work was up against this. He thought there would be some change. Pinching his nose, he took a few deep breaths. His youngest grandson came to mind. The boy twin who was sensitive to his surroundings and also a Bi-Genetic. Rage consumed him. If any of those bastards touched him. He let the thought dissipate.

"We got to figure out how to nip this thing in the ass," he said more to himself.

"Well, we know the people behind it," the second said while driving.

Hoskins sucked air in through gritted teeth. He had helped them out as a way to show the organization they had no control. Now he wanted to go in and tear that room apart. And then tear each sector leader new assholes. There would be no good sleep for him tonight.

~

Kevin sat on his own porch in an old school white wooden rocking chair sipping from a bottle of beer. In the matching chair next to him was Hoskins staring off into the distance. He sympathized with the former General after he too received surveillance from all four sectors. Napalm came to mind every time he scrolled through the feeds. The two men had been sitting without speaking for a while now, not sure how to even begin.

His middle son had no issues within the community because he made sure all his children were combat trained. One of the liaison people had approached him two years ago about his son and he respectfully declined, with an old school 9mm Glock locked and loaded within reach the entire conversation. He too could never have imagined what he had seen.

"Suggestions?" Kevin finally asked.

"No idea how to even start," Hoskins replied.

"What?" Kevin turned his head to him. "You, the man always looking to obstruct government agendas?"

"Yeah, when I knew what the hell they were after. This shit makes no sense at all."

"Of course it does. This is how humanity has been since the Roman empire and beyond. Think there's an end game plan?"

"Absolutely!, And I want in."

Kevin snorted and took another swig of his beer. The whole thing was an atrocity and he wondered what the architects of this project were doing.

~

Soft kisses being planted all over woke Hana from a deep sleep. Always in female form when at home, she relished the morning ritual. Her husband's lips caressed her ear.

"You're so pretty," he whispered. "And soft. So cuddly."

She suppressed a giggle, so he wouldn't know she was indeed awake. He nuzzled her neck and she instinctively scrunched up. There went that charade. He kissed the back of her neck and smacked her hard on the side of her ass before getting up. She heard the shower turn on in the bathroom. Not ready to get up yet, Hana just laid in bed staring at the wall. Weight pushed down on her, slowly creeping up until a small body sat in front of her, arms rocking her with each push. Her gaze slid over to her five-year-old son.

"Momma, up. Want outside and play."

She pulled him close to her, taking in his scent.

Someone had bathed him.

Fine tuning her hearing, she could make out

movement in the kitchen. Only one person came this early in the morning unannounced. Reluctant to leave the warmth of the covers, she maneuvered sideways, scooting out with her son clinging tight until her feet touched the floor. She set him down and he raced off ahead of her.

The kitchen was spotless yet her eldest son stood at the breakfast bar eating a bowl of oatmeal clearly made only moments ago. He wore scrubs underneath a white lab coat, his hospital badge half hidden by the way he leaned over. His Asian features were subtle so many people speculated wrong about his ethnicity. He got his height from his father, standing at a little over six feet tall.

"Is that the only reason you come around?" She asked, nodding at the bowl.

He simply looked up at her then took another spoonful of his breakfast. His father came into the room wearing drawstring pants and a towel wrapped around his neck. Both men gave each other a nod of acknowledgement.

"Oh, he just likes to antagonize us on occasion."

Their son dropped his spoon into the bowl and stood straight. Before he could say anything, the second oldest came speeding through wearing fatigues. A handful of fruit was grabbed along with a bottle of premixed energy drink.

"Oh, shit!" He said breathlessly, glancing at the microwave clock, and was out the door.

Hana glanced at her husband.

"I am not his commander."

He saw the time on the counter then went to the refrigerator.

"Can we address the elephant in the room?" Her eldest asked.

"And what would that be?"

"Oh, you know. The organization a mess, your little social experiment about to implode and the fact that an alien race is coming to wipe us off the face of our solar system in what, a little over a decade?" Hana frowned, and her husband halted drinking from a carton at the open refrigerator door. "I don't have the same kind of faith in humanity getting it together in the last hours like you do."

"We can't curl into a ball and wish it all away," Hans answered.

The five-year-old came running in and stopped near his big brother.

"And this," he said staring down on the little boy. "Seriously, stop." Hana felt her face flush with anger. "It's irresponsible considering the situation." He picked up his youngest brother and set him on top of the breakfast bar in front of him. The little boy wrapped his arms around his neck. "I'd take him away from you if I could."

"Say what?" His father asked angrily.

Hana couldn't move out of guilt. She knew her son was right in a way.

Their oldest held the boy tighter.

"But I know that would make him sad and don't want to hurt any of us."

His little brother raised his head up.

"Wanna' go play."

"Yeah? Alright."

He lifted the boy up to set him back down on the floor.

"Don't you have to go back to work?" Hana asked.

"Section upgrade. Four hours."

"Oh."

"Another advance in medical technology that won't do us any good in the long run."

For once, Hana wanted to hear something positive. Everyone was so focused on the bad when there was some good being done. The organization wasn't a complete failure. Rule number one in any strategy, always have a plan B, C, and D.

An emergency meeting to take place inside Neil's office in Sector One was called for the architects. Stan and Reimer were already there with Hana. General Perrara came up to Neil as he walked through the building's front doors. Side by side, they headed for the elevators. Neither spoke the entire ride up. The sliding doors opened to the meeting area situated before Neil's desk. A conference table that could seat six sat in the middle.

Hana, in male form, was already seated, perusing the data on his tablet via a holoscreen. Stan and Reimer were huddled together in heated whispers, their foreheads wrinkled. General Perrara took a deep breath and made his way to the table. He was not looking his sharpest, in a casual shirt and jeans. His hair had not been coifed to perfection due to time. Not a good start in his eyes.

"So," he started.

"Well?" Stan asked wearily.

"What a fuck up!" Reimer said.

Hana rested his head in one hand, covering his face. There was no denying that.

"Yes, genius, we figured that out! Hence, the meeting." Neil replied.

"Let's not start the blame game. We dropped the ball," Perrara chided.

"We were blindsided," Reimer added.

"Now what?" Hana asked.

Perrara scratched his head, messing up his hair more. He knew what needed to be done would make him seem like a dog with its tail between its legs begging forgiveness. Hana's stare solidified the notion for he too appeared defeated.

"All in favor of plan C?"

"What?" Reimer cried out.

"What happened to plan B?"

"Oh, we've gone way past that option," Stan stated.

Everyone else raised their hands and waited for Reimer to do the same.

"May there be mercy on our souls." Reimer finally raised his hand.

"We don't get to ask for mercy on this one," Neil retorted.

CHAPTER TWO

FACTION OF FACILITIES

The floating artificial island was in the middle of nowhere in the ocean surrounded by a milky dome. A closer pass by the plane revealed it was a barrier. On board were the architects of the grid community along with two representatives from each sector. Neil had handpicked them, circumventing the sector heads and the liaisons who were the reason for the cities mess. They had been briefed and set to task on finding all related data. He had given over the reins to the grid after a couple of years, confident his set up would suffice. All the architects had done so and now here they were, trying to repair the damage.

General Perrara sat near a window lost in his own reverie. He had finally told them about his arrangement with Professor Bartley. After a full week of heated arguments, temper tantrums and accusations flying, they all agreed it was the best option. Neil didn't envy him. He scanned the cabin and felt impressed. Stan was dressed in a high-end suit, looking equal to Reimer. All the representatives were in business attire, including himself, and the General was in his dress blues. They all wanted to make sure the facility leaders understood their convictions.

"Please return to your seats and secure for landing," the pilot's voice came over the system.

They did as instructed and waited to arrive on the island. From his window, Neil saw the barrier open to a massive structure on the far end. It gleamed in the sunlight like a white beacon amid the forests. There were smaller structures that he could barely make out because they blended so well into the environment. A lit runway of flashing orbs appeared out of nowhere below, leading straight to the white building. The other side of it protruded out into the ocean then down.

What the hell? He asked himself.

A smooth landing and they hurried out of their seats to step out onto the tarmac once the doors opened. Ocean air hit them in the face and Neil was the only one who stopped to breath it in. Years of working in a desert let him appreciate water more. He drank in the atmosphere then suddenly halted his pleasure. Looking around he found no guards, no defensive artillery; nothing. No one had come to greet them either. Instead there was a pathway with instructions on how to get to the main entrance. He turned to General Perrara who also seemed perturbed.

"Well, let's get this show on the road," Reimer called out.

He strolled down the ramp and led the way. Feeling uneasy, Neil followed with the others behind him. Beautiful landscaping lined the path on both sides. There had to be at least thirty different flowers producing the light floral scent that hung in the air. Sounds of wildlife was all around and Neil swore he saw what appeared to be a Toucan lounging in a tree above. Up ahead was the entrance to the main building. A young man who looked of teenage years paced slowly in front of it. When the entourage approached, he stopped and stared at them.

Eyes hollow of everything. No emotions, no acknowledgement, empty. Neil had seen those before from some of the trainees. This kid's demeanor was from something else, not torture. As he got closer, it dawned on him what it resembled; loss.

"Welcome to Facility HQ," the kid deadpanned. "Please follow me."

They followed him through the double doors that opened automatically without keycard or password. While the doors were still open, a wildcat jumped onto the path and made a beeline for them. The kid turned and raised one hand to the entrance. In seconds, the wildcat crashed into an invisible barrier, a whine escaping its mouth before being tossed back in the dense foliage. That was his answer to the lack of security. Doors closed, they all proceeded.

Walls, floors, and ceiling were pure white, even the furniture. There were no doors, and he knew from visiting facility three that they could appear anywhere. Perrara kept in stride with him, the rest of the group having fallen back. He watched the kid take calculated steps in a sort of off rhythm which in turn almost threw off his own. After walking for what seemed like minutes, the kid halted and faced the wall on the left. Thin lines formed in a rectangle and the white disappeared to reveal an entrance. Inside, the corridor was a light cream color. Neil let his vision adjust to the change.

They loaded up in an elevator not fifty feet away and the kid pressed a button. The buttons had symbols instead of numbers, the higher ones accompanied with tiny sensors for scanning. When the elevator stopped, it opened to a huge room with a conference table that took up most of it. Floor to ceiling windows lined the entire left side, giving a view of the island and ocean. Straight ahead was a giant vidscreen taking up the wall. Seated at the table were twenty men and women, some in lab coats.

"I brought them," the kid said, scratching the side of his nose with a finger.

"Thank you, Brian. Please go back to your station."

A man Neil had never seen before stood up and waved him away. The kid pivoted in military style and left the room.

"Boring," the kid complained on his way out.

All eyes fell on the entourage and Neil felt apprehension coming from them. Now he knew why General Perrara didn't want to be point on this meeting. These were not the facility owners they had a rapport with.

"Please, have a seat. Let's begin." The same man gestured to the table.

"Should we do introductions?" Neil asked as his group took their seats.

"No need. We know who you are. Professor Bartley has given us a rather brief insight into the nature of this meeting, but we would like to hear it from you."

"Alright." Neil's hands started to clam up, so he did a sly wipe across his lap before setting them on the table. "You may have heard about the community we constructed some years ago." There were a few nods. "We had high hopes of changing the atmosphere regarding hostility towards Bi-Genetics."

"And you have failed," a female stated loudly.

Neil sat back at the verbal assault.

"We have hit a snag, yes," he continued.

"Nonetheless, a failure," a man in a lab coat added.

Reimer slapped a hand on the table, getting their attention.

"You don't need to reiterate that fact! Are we going to talk like adults, or what?"

The room went tense and Neil could feel their disdain. Leave it to the assistant secretary to pick a fight at the worst time.

"My apologies," Neil said. "It is a very sensitive subject. We had every hope of this project succeeding."

"Humans cannot change in so short a time."

A differnt man from the opposite side said.

"So," the first man began. "What are we dealing with?"

With a nod from Neil, the sector representatives pulled out their tablets and set them on the conference table. Blue lines raced across the surface as the vidscreen came to life and they all looked up at the data. This was also the first time he and the other architects had seen it, so he couldn't stifle the gasp that escaped him. He clutched both hands together and forced his eyes not to squeeze shut.

"What are these?" A woman on the far end cried out.

"Good God!" The man across from her exclaimed.

Images of people, graphs, and charts flooded the vidscreen, overlapping each other. General Perrara made a fist and averted his gaze. Minutes went by as the facility members went through the data. The first man finally looked over at him.

"What is the meaning of these missing persons?"

"You mean deceased," a woman next to him interjected.

"There is no evidence," Neil started to say.

"That is partially correct," the third sector representative replied. "This is part of our crime statistics and there is indication that many of the missing are presumed dead."

"What are you saying?" Neil snapped. "The population has remained steady."

"Only because we filled the empty areas with waitlist candidates over the years."

Neil's face sagged in comprehension. He had created the waitlist for cases when contracts were violated, and the families had to be booted out.

"Where are the bodies?" The facilitator asked.

"No idea. We suspect," the second sector rep said, "they have been harvested somehow."

"Compared to the ones who were indeed removed from the community, what percentage are we talking?"

"Of the population, eight percent have been documented removals. Thirty two percent are in the missing category." The fourth representative replied.

"Mostly children," the woman in the lab coat said.

"Unfortunately, yes."

"And what are we to do?" The facilitator asked.

This time General Perrara spoke. He sat straight in his seat.

"We need a purge. Professor Bartley has assured me that if it came to this, we would have your full cooperation."

"A purge? That entails what?"

"We leave it up to you."

"Oh?" Another man leaned forward on the table, his stare that of a monster. "Is that wise? Your Shadow Organization has quite a reputation. We are an anomaly."

The way his eyes never shifted, bearing down on the General, frightened Neil, and he feared nothing. He began to question if this was indeed the right thing to do.

"Yes, you should have done that first," the man said.

Neil and the rest of his group simultaneously scooted back from the table in shock. Their chairs made loud screeches that echoed through the room. He immediately blocked off his mind with a technique Celestial Mother had taught him. The man frowned at him.

Not happening, you monster!

It wasn't the fact that he was a telepath. Neil had experienced plenty over the decades. No. This was an ultimate intrusion. A stealth and speed he had never encountered. He felt danger ooze from the man's demeanor.

"Let's not use intimidation tactics," the facilitator chided the man. When the room became more relaxed and the group scooted forward to the table, he resumed the meeting. "I think we should take this step by step. This is going to be a long day."

Every piece of data was scrutinized and explained throughout the day with an hour and a half lunch break consisting of gourmet fare on white plates. By late afternoon, Neil was mentally exhausted. The data was copied to the facility's server and he was anxious for his group to be on its way. There were still no introductions. Through observation and conversations, he had learned a few names and that the facilitator was also the Chairman.

"Ladies, gentlemen," the facilitator said. "This has been enlightening. I am sure you are eager to return home. Once a plan has been approved, we will contact you."

"That's fine by me," Reimer snorted. "Let's get the hell out of here."

Neil sighed in defeat. There was no pulling the reins on that man.

Back on the plane, Neil turned to the sector representatives.

"Bodies! Harvesting! You better explain that shit to me, right now!"

They all flinched away from him.

Hana, who had been quiet the entire time all day, placed a hand on his chest to stop him from leaning forward. They locked eyes and he finally understood. It was no longer in their hands. They had waved the white flag and accepted a new fate.

The Chairman walked over to one of the windows and watched his guests' plane take off. His colleagues sat continuing their analysis of the data. This was a strange turn of events. One that the facilities would never had anticipated. Over the decades, owners of each facility began to see their separatism as detrimental to the goal.

The Shadow Organization's blunder opened a doorway. He turned back to address the room.

"We will have to take this slow."

"Yes," the telepath said. "This is a delicate matter."

"The missing is what disturbs me. Someone knows something about this and not telling the higher ups."

"That is curious." The facilitator came closer to the table. "What do you think?" He asked the telepath.

"Hana. That one knows. He may not have known how it tied into this, but he does now. The man didn't even flinch when that was revealed."

"That was a man?" The female scientist was incredulous. "I'm losing my edge."

Some of the others laughed.

"Before we dive in and create recommendations, we need more information."

"This isn't enough?" A male scientist asked. "We've only brushed the surface of this. It's going to take months to really dig in deep."

The telepath sat back in his seat and a sinister grin formed. He swayed the chair back side to side while his fingers rubbed together in the air above his ear.

"I think," he said. "I know where to look."

The gleam in his eyes let the Chairman know he was on the right trail. He always found what he was looking for. Even when it didn't want to be.

Hoskins Sr. strolled through his near empty house enjoying the silence. His grandson had finally been deployed after years of bureaucratic bullshit based on his father's actions. No one wanted the son of a traitor in their midst. The eldest child, his granddaughter had fought tooth and nail to keep her rank and stay in the military. She was a force to be reckoned with and

Hoskins felt his grandson should have taken her cue.

Gets that from my damnable son, Hoskins thought.

His right-hand man came into the living room where he had ended up.

"Where is he?" Hoskins asked.

"In the wind but not for long. We got a lead but it's the way he got it."

"Hmm?" Hoskins was intrigued. His son had escaped being killed numerous times now and was sure it wasn't due to fate. There was an agenda to keep him alive, for now. "And what did the trick?"

"Terrors. A few turned on him and didn't follow."

"He underestimated them. I knew those things could wipe us all off the face of the planet if given the chance. That's why I had fail-safes in place."

"True, boss. That incident was probably the catalyst."

"And for some reason the rest of the organization is not in the know."

"Can't blame the kid for trying."

Hoskins tsked. Hana was no kid anymore and far from helpless. He had a destructive talent that wasn't powerful enough for his use but deadly all the same.

"Come to think of it, he knew I was here."

"I told you, you'd stick out."

He waved a hand at him and went to the window. Across the way and down the street, he saw Kevin sitting on his porch in a daze. That look meant he was thinking of something not particular nice. Whoever the poor bastard might be, Hoskins felt a little sorry for them. Nevertheless, Kevin had become a great partner and asset to the cause. Kevin's stare turned on him and from that distance, the two men agreed on the next step.

⌐

Clouds thickening, in the sky, grew darker, signaling rain. Sunset had begun, and the grid community was eerily silent. People bustled about as usual amid a dark curtain drawn over them. Neil declared it as deep shame. They knew what was going on and were starting to feel sickened by their own depravity. In his office on the highest point of the monolith, he watched them with animosity. The first pelts of rain hit the windows and he stood arms crossed, wrinkling the sleeves of his dark suit. His hair had gotten long over the years, hanging past his shoulders, and he had no intention of cutting it. That was the last thing on his mind in terms of urgency.

"Contact the City Attorney," he called out to the A.I.

"Contacting. Stand by."

"Voice only."

"Confirmed."

He waited patiently.

"This is Sector Three. What can I do for you?"

"Get your ass down to my office," Neil replied.

"That's uncalled for. I won't be berated into whatever your sick brain has in mind."

"I would like you," Neil seethed, "to come down to my office for a meeting."

"In regard to what?"

"You know what! I'm not going to spew it on an open channel!"

"Oh." The was silence on the other end. "I will be there within the hour."

"And bring me all," Neil emphasized the last word," of the missing persons data."

"I will do that. See you soon."

The connection died, and he pinched the bridge of his nose. Everything about it stunk and he was going to get to the bottom of it.

Right on time, the city attorney arrived at the monolith and was escorted to him. Neil scrutinized the man briefly, having not assess him thoroughly on previous occasions. That was sloppiness on his part and unlike himself. At closer observation, the Sector Three representative was plain; unassuming. Spy. He knew a few of them would have gotten in under the radar.

"So, tell me." He gestured for him to sit as he did the same. "How did you ever find out about the harvesting?"

"Process of elimination. Tip offs and rumors."

"From where and who?" Neil couldn't read the man's eyes. There was no wavering or a glitch in demeanor. A true solid agent. "That's a big leap from missing to something so egregious as body parts for sale." He leaned forward. "Who are you, really?"

"A direct hire for Hana. Just call me Agent X."

He could feel the heat rise in his face and knew he was turning flushed. Agent X cracked a smile, making him angrier. Hana was appearing to have more clout in the organization than him and he was one of the best trainers.

What did I miscalculate?

"I see you trying to figure out the details," Agent X said. "But if Hana doesn't want you to know, then you don't."

"That is not an option! We are in a crisis, here."

"True. But we are no longer in charge."

"Until those facility chairmen come to us with details, we will try to correct this ourselves."

Agent X let out a sigh and handed his tablet over to him.

"This is all of it. Don't beat yourself in the head over this too much. You will have a part to play regardless what happens." He stood up to leave.

"Don't you need this back?"

"It's a disposable one. I have many."

Of course you do, he scoffed inwardly as the spy left his office.

He remained at his desk scouring the tablet, his mind refusing to accept it and whatever contents it held. His trust level had plummeted in the last few months.

Hana.

"What game are you playing, you shitty little half breed?"

☙

Jungles were fascinating on their own except Hoskins Jr's affinity for them bordered on addiction. There the man was, surrounded by a new crew of guerilla soldiers, hell bent on saving their race through unfounded means. The uniforms this time were grey fatigues with tan combat boots. In the grass hut constructed near the main building, Hoskins Jr. laughed loudly with his men. He had abandoned his new family long ago, leaving them to face death.

The telepath despised the man. He was ten times worse than his father. A Terror patrolling the compound's border stopped in his view and turned to stare at him. Neither man made a move. The Terror smirked and continued his patrol.

So, they're not even going to warn him there's an intruder?

For what purpose? The Terror invaded his mind.

Aren't you supposed to protect him? The telepath was uneasy.

Are you here to harm him?

Maybe. Then he thought about it. *No, just gathering information.*

Then we don't have a problem.

When the Terror left his viewpoint, the telepath made his way back to the camp site he had propped up a half mile away. He would have to devise a plan to get one of the diehard soldiers who had fled with Hoskins for interrogation. If the Terrors in his ranks were like the one he encountered then his chances were good.

By night time, the air was less muggy, yet he still had to strip down to only his thermal cooling tank top and cargo pants. His boots lay by him while he let his feet get some circulation. He mindlessly whittled a piece of bark into what resembled a frog. His gaze fixated on the guerilla compound off in the distance. A stare devoid of emotion.

I might have to kill some of these whack jobs, he thought.

Except Hoskins Jr. Not yet.

Three law enforcement vehicles came screeching to a halt in front of Kevin's house. He stood up from checking the condition of his lawn with his hands and cocked his head back. The vehicles emptied out and eight people converged on his property. One of the four men in suits approached him in a huff.

"I need you to come with me, sir." The last word was spat out vehemently. "Your cooperation is mandatory."

Out of the corner of his eye, Kevin saw Hoskins Sr. standing outside watching. A dark look was planted on his face and he signaled with his gaze to not interfere, yet.

"Mandatory? By whom?" Kevin wiped his hands on the back of his pants.

The men in suits looked around at the neighbors coming out to see what was going on.

"It would behoove you to not make a scene."

"A scene?"

A bright swirl of light flashed in Kevin's eyes and

the first man halted his advance in dread. Strong wind rushed through the air. The sky turned nearly black, clouds churning into a funnel. Lightning came down, striking cars, trees and houses. The ground shifted. Cracks formed down the black top and rose up to open a way to hell below. Neighbors ran back into their houses screaming. Hoskins and his crew remain looking on from the porch.

Then it all stopped. The ground receded back, and the sky cleared.

"The only ones making a scene are you and the more than necessary back up."

The other men in suits along with the officers stepped back away from his property line, leaving their leader fear bound in front of him.

"My employers humbly request your presence at a meeting scheduled today."

The man nervously licked his lips.

"And who are your employers?"

The man leaned closer and whispered, "The architects."

Kevin burst out laughing. When he was done, he glanced over at Hoskins and winked. An update was imminent. He would go see what the 'architects' wanted.

Usually, when a faction of humans did something stupid, Darnizva would go and have a talk with them about being more proactive in the upcoming war. Finding out Celestial Mother had somehow gotten involved called for a new plan. He had been suspicious of her motives over the years and already saw through her end game agenda. Intel he received gave him the location of a meeting being held within the grid community and he decided to make a surprise appearance.

The layout was as reported, and he could feel the tension in the air. Every place he traveled had the same vibe filled with negativity. His ship coasted above the tallest buildings towards the monolith in the middle. Residents below looked up in awe at his arrival. He switched on the autopilot and let it land the craft onto the parking lot's black top. Security guards scrambled to surround it, albeit hesitantly.

A man in a suit came running out of the building and stood next to the ship, waiting for him to come out. Darnizva tapped the hatch release and jumped down beside him.

"Captain Darnizva. It's quite a surprise to see you." The man seemed nervous.

"Yes, well." He ran his fingers through his thick mane of hair. "You left me no choice, didn't you?"

The man sputtered before finally speaking.

"We are handling this."

Darnizva frowned, his cinnamon colored irises growing brighter until they were blood red.

"That's the problem." He stared down at the man. "Would you be so kind as to show me the way?" The man's face scrunched up. "Take me to your leader," Darnizva ordered. The man snapped to attention in fright.

"Of course. Please follow me."

As he was escorted into the building, Darnizva laughed inwardly. He'd always wanted to say that after watching so many of Earth's science fiction films.

The meeting room was full, the atmosphere grim. Neil was none too happy about Darnizva being there. Hana, in female form, kept her head down. Her belly appeared larger than her whole body and she had to be uncomfortable in the rounded seat. All the players were present, so Neil sat down at the end of the table to commence the agenda.

"Thank you all for coming." He eyed Darnizva. "Captain, a pleasure."

"Don't thank me just yet. What you say here determines my mood going forward."

"Fair enough."

"Before we go any further, I want to know about this whole harvesting business."

"Of course. That is the main reason for this meeting."

Agent X cleared his throat and looked around the room.

"We were able to find the distributor, but he got away. At least we now know the details of what was going on."

"And how did you address the issue?" Darnizva asked.

"There was a mission," Hana whispered.

Four Months Earlier

For the second time, Erica found someone she didn't want anything to do with standing at her front door. Cast in a halo from the midday sun and wearing a three-piece suit, Neil Shannon smiled wide at her. Behind him was Hana looking out of sorts in a more casual yet no less expensive one. The overly beautiful man managed a grimace.

"Why? What do you want from me now?" She asked in defeat.

"May we come in? It would be best not to discuss it out in the open," Neil said.

She reluctantly opened the door wider and stepped aside for them to enter. A quick surveillance of the neighbors assured her no one was watching. Ever since the extraction incident, they had become increasingly nosy about her actions.

Hana and Neil sat down on the sofa, both unbuttoning their jackets for comfort.

"So, what is it?" She plopped down on the matching sofa across from them.

Neil leaned forward.

"We're not here to beat around the bush. We need your assistance with a side mission."

"I am not in play at the moment," she replied.

"You are a Shadow agent. You are always in play."

She gripped the fabric of her pants, forming creases in her lap.

"I am sure you've heard about the Grid Community," Hana stated.

"So stupid," she said. "How could you do something like that?"

Hana became visibly upset. Before he could say anything in return, Neil placed a hand on his shoulder.

"It was done with all the best intentions. Things didn't turn out as expected, is all."

"And?"

Hana cleared his throat and regained his composure.

"We have found there is an underground harvesting of bodies for Bi-Genetic DNA within the cities."

She fell back against the sofa in shock.

"Children?"

"Since Bi-Genetics are products of their parents," Hana said darkly. "Them, as well."

"That's sickening. Why do you need me?"

"I am setting up a meeting to negotiate with the person at the root cause."

"We need a hand to hand combat specialist who's also a gun expert along with a few others," Neil added.

"Who is this person?"

The two men hesitated.

She felt a sudden boulder drop in the pit of her

stomach and knew before Hana blurted it out.

"Your ex-husband, the former General."

"Who is constantly hiding in some jungle or another," Neil said.

"Why should I go and see that monster again?"

"Because," he replied, smiling. "This time there's no need for you to hold back."

She looked at the grin on his face and at Hana's unease.

"This is what you want?" She asked Hana.

"I want him to see reason and for this mission not to turn into blood bath. But," Hana stopped.

"He won't," she said flatly.

"I have to at least try. It's been years, and no one has assassinated him yet. He should feel relaxed."

"All the more reason why he has no fear of you, or me." She got up and went to the liquor cabinet. "I don't know about you, but I need a drink first."

⤳

Hana had no intention of backing down from the former general. He wanted to make it clear to the man that his actions would not be tolerated any longer. Aboard the air transport ship were Erica, Shannon, Damon Peterson, Agent X, himself, and his husband, Scott. All of them were dressed in green fatigues minus Damon who wore a long black coat over dress shirt and slacks. He had been retrieved while on police duty and had refused to change.

Stubborn as ever.

The transport circled above the dense jungle until the copilot tapped the pilot and pointed. It sped through the air, getting closer to the village now visible below. From their distance, Hana could see two men atop a land to air missile launcher aimed straight at them. Hoskins walked up behind them and made a motion to move out. Not seeming very happy about it, the two men retreated. Hana breathed a sigh of relief. He didn't want the transport to try out its amazing maneuver capabilities while inside.

Hana drove a hard bargain to get Erica on board with his idea and he didn't blame her for wanting no part. Chad Hoskins was a monster in every way as she claimed. Harder still was convincing Celestial Mother to agree on letting Damon accompany them, let alone bring the special made sword only a few agents could wield.

"Where do you want to land, sir?" The pilot asked through the headset comm.

"Not too close." He turned to the experts riding with him and waited for a suggestion.

"There would be good," Scott said, pointing to a clearing a quarter mile from the village.

The pilot turned his head to follow Scott's finger.

"Roger that. Prepare for landing."

The transport glided smoothly down towards the spot.

At the clearing, Hana stepped out and scoped his surroundings, the military trained doing the same. Hana had learned a few things over the years despite being a desk jockey. The trees were close knit around them, nearly blocking the sunlight. A few rays filtered through and the heat was not yet at its peak. Insects buzzed, and birds cawed.

One of the soldiers slapped his arm hard, killing a bug that had landed.

"Hate the friggin jungle," he muttered.

"I need Peterson and you two," Scott wiggled two fingers at the soldiers in the rear, "to stay here in case shit hits the fan. We aren't too far away for you to come get us if necessary."

"Then what was the purpose of me coming and

bringing that thing?" Damon nodded over at the specially made sword wrapped in cloth lying on the transport floor.

"I am hoping we don't need it."

"You really expect Hoskins to agree with your terms?" Scott asked.

"I'd like to think he could still see reason."

"You're still asking a lot," Erica said in a defeated tone.

"Like I said. All I can do is try. Come on, let's get this over with."

Two of the soldiers took point, rifles ready, and led the way through the foliage. Hana, Neil and Erica were center with Scott and Agent X covering the rear. As they approached, a group of guerilla fighters ran up to surround them, blocking the way back. Up ahead, Hoskins Jr. sat leisurely under a straw roofed structure, his personal Terror across from him. The Terror wore a cream-colored seersucker suit with a tight-fitting muscle tee underneath. His short blond hair and almond colored eyes were in contrast with the vicious stare he gave them. Seeing Hana and his ex, Hoskins began to lightly snort while laughing.

"Well, holy shit!" He got up and walked towards them. "The little girly boy and my cunt of a wife."

"I'm no longer your wife," she snapped.

"Nah, you went and hooked up with that doctor who patched you up. Desperate much?"

Hana saw her hands ball into fists and moved close to her side.

"Are you done?" Hana said with authority.

That made Hoskins' head snap back in surprise.

"You getting uppity with me, femboy?"

The fighters around him raised their weapons and Hana's soldiers followed suit.

"I didn't come here for a fight," Hana cried out.

"Yeah? Then why did you?"

"Your underground harvest trade. It needs to cease from now on."

Hoskins let out a hearty laugh that went on for longer than it should. He suddenly stopped and gave them a hateful glare.

"Their organs would have been discarded anyway. What the hell do you care about dead bodies?"

"Because you are selling them on the black market."

"Everybody wants to extend their life and willing to pay big money for it. Not my fault that alien DNA works wonders."

"We will not allow you to do that anymore."

"You know what?" Hoskins began to step back.

"Move!" Erica ordered Hana who looked over at her confused.

"Kill em," Hoskins said with a smile.

Even though they were in close proximity, Scott and the two soldiers were able to dodge flying bullets as the guerilla fighters in the area opened fire. Erica grabbed Hana in the nick of time and pushed him down to the ground. He tasted the sandy dirt as it dusted up into his mouth. Four fighters came at them and Erica jumped up for defense. With speed and case, she took them out one by one. Her first gun came out when she had enough distance to aim without delay. She switched effortlessly between grappling and shooting. Mesmerized by her expertise, Hana forgot he was left open.

Hoskins's Terror grabbed him by the ankle, dragging him closer until he was directly beneath the behemoth. Before Hana could defend himself, the Terror dropped a hard blow to his chest. All the air went out of him and for a split second he couldn't breathe. He knew that pain. Some of his ribs were broken. Hana managed to turn over and tried crawling away. The Terror continued to land a series of blows, even kicks to his sides. One perfect hit to the stomach forced an instant shift into female form, leaving Hana's body momentarily weak. A loud heartbeat thumped in Hana's ear and filled with dread, she cried.

Oh no! No, no!

She hadn't been feeling good, never once thinking the obvious answer as to why. Frightened, Hana fought desperately to claw her way to safety. The Terror, seemingly bored, turned away having done enough damage. Each attempt to catch her breath resulted in a blood-spattered cough. Four of Hoskins's fighters separated from the main fight and converged on her, one pulled on her pants while another held her head down to the ground. Her vision blurred from teary eyes as she realized what her fate was about to entail. With a primal scream, Hana unleash a maelstrom of energy that threw her assailants off and into the jungle trees.

The Terror had found a new plaything in Shannon. As fast as Neil was, he still got wounded quicker than he thought. His hand to hand combat specialty was nowhere near the same level as the Terror. Not willing to back down, he got ready to advance on the Terror and found himself already out of the fight, flying backwards through the air. He could taste blood flooding his esophagus as he slammed against a tree. The Terror then turned his attention elsewhere. His fingers became long, sharp talons that when struck together caused a spark. He sliced through two of Hana's soldiers and a slew of Hoskins's men to get to Erica. While she still fought the guerillas, he cut them open as well and tossed them aside.

From his position near the hut where he was engaged with four guerillas, Agent X saw Hoskins's eyes go wide with fear. The man probably never took into consideration that the Terror he had obtained was a nut job. The worst kind of killer who feigned loyalty. Hoskins slowly moved towards his transport on the other side of the village. A small group of fighters followed. He ignored the cries of his wife and daughter as he fled past them to preserve his own life. Even as they ran after him, the transport shut its doors and began lift off.

Agent X cursed himself. He saw the Terror go after Hana and could do nothing since a group of Hoskins's men came at him. The first one got almost on him while he was distracted until he came to realize his predicament and snapped the man's neck. from there, it was a battle.

Right as the Terror reached Erica, Damon appeared between them, stopping the giant man in his tracks. Neither man budged, staring each other down. They broke at the same time and Damon went into a defensive stance, sword held low behind him. The Terror cracked his neck on both sides and grinned.

"Shadowman."

"Yeah. Come get some."

The two men clashed at such high speeds, their body movements were a blur of lights. Claws and sword created sparks on contact. Damon saw an opening and went for it. To his surprise, the Terror managed to somersault backwards, barely missing the swing of his blade. It sliced clean through a large boulder behind him.

"Awwrrr! Keep still, you bastard," Damon shouted. He pulled the sword up and it met the Terrors claws again. "Oh? You are a fast one."

"Gonna' rip you apart. See what's inside," the Terror sneered.

Damon managed to get free and had to fend off the rapid succession of blows the Terror kept delivering. He had already received a few deep cuts and that made him angry. With a wide swing, he forced the Terror to maneuver out of the way. When he spun around to launch himself at Damon, he pivoted to the right and swung his blade upwards between the Terror's legs. Like an invisible light, the blade appeared from the top of the Terror's head as Damon stood sideways before him. Still held up in the air, a single drop of blood slid down the blade.

The fighting stopped

Hoskins's men fell back in fear, scrambling to escape. The Terror stood still, not sure if he should try to move or not. His eyes went blank. Scott was able to get to where Erica had Hana's head in her lap to keep her from choking on her own blood. Hana watched a thin seam of red form upwards on the Terror's back up to his head. Erica clamped a hand over her eyes.

"No! Don't look!"

Damon and Agent X were now side by side assessing the area. A thump like heavy rock on sand followed by another was heard. Damon was about to turn his head.

"Don't," Agent X admonished. "There's no need to confirm. Let's get our people and go. A second team is on the way for cleanup."

With her hand still covering Hana's view, Erica and Scott lifted then carried her towards the transport. High above, they could all hear Hoskins's ship speeding off into the distance.

"There's no way we can follow him now." Neil shuffled to them.

"Goddamnit!!" Damon whacked the tip of his sword on the ground.

Surrounded by carnage, those still alive screaming in pain and rage, the ragtag group admitted defeat.

ᔪ

The story finished, Darnizva could feel his face tighten as he struggled to contain himself. His eyes burned, and he knew they were glowing red with anger. He couldn't fathom what went through humans' minds when it came to such things. Even in his race's darkest hours, they had never fallen so deep as that.

DEVISING A PLAN

Neil's lips twitched at the sides until a smile formed. In his mind, a new plan was forming. It was a daunting endeavor that would also put his other expertise back in play; assassination tactics. The Shadow Organization was too flashy. What he required were tried and true government killers kept under the radar. There was one slight snag. He would have to tap some of his government buddies to acquire them. Which also meant the President would be advised.

A devious thought came to him. Involving the United States in this mess would put them in the spotlight. When the shit hits the fan, they would take the blame. He decided to contact the facility headquarters and inform them of a few extra incoming agents.

The facilities chairman stood with hands clasped behind his back at conference room's floor to ceiling windows. His entire staff waited for his feedback on their proposal submissions. Seated around the overly large table, they glanced around at each other trying to gauge the mood. He could feel their angst. This was no small task. For the plan to work, hundreds of operatives would need to be activated. He sighed, his shoulders sagging a bit, before turning to face them.

"Are there any concerns about the numbers presented?" he asked.

One of the scientists stood to answer.

"None. We believe twenty-five agents is more than enough."

An office manager also stood to speak.

"Infiltration and reconfiguration of the main systems should only require ten."

The chairman stepped to the head of the table.

"That's fine. What I want to know is if the method and body count is acceptable."

He saw many of them frown, the others' expressions were malicious.

"Ridding the planet of bottom feeders like those is a necessity," his secretary blurted.

"What about Shannon's proposal?" He directed his question towards Talbot.

The telepath swiveled side to side in his chair, deep in thought. When he raised his head up, the look in his eyes said plenty. He was not too happy.

"There is no question, the U.S. government will get wind of this along the way. I don't trust their operatives."

"Even if they were planted by our organization?" The chairman asked.

"That's dangerous. We could be seen negatively for it."

"Oh, who gives a good goddamn?" A female lab tech yelled as she slammed a fist down. "If they don't know by now that Bi-Genetics are embedded everywhere in society, then I have no respect for them."

"She has a point," the office manager said.

"Timeline?" His secretary asked.

"The quicker, the better," the scientist replied.

"Let's make sure all of the logistics are in order. We will reconvene in one week." The chairman nodded to them, signaling dismissal.

Everyone walked out of the room except Talbot, back in his own mind.

The Chairman went up the steps leading to the window facing the main roadway. From there he could see most of the island. Nothing stirred in the horizon. Peaceful as always. He stepped down from the platform below the windows and walked towards the telepath.

"What have you found out so far?"

The telepath finally smiled, his lips a thin line.

"Shannon has indeed tapped a faction of the government where Shadow members are in place. He's under the impression that there is some loyalty among them."

"Oh?"

"By doing this, he has also piqued the interest of the President and she is now throwing her own agents in the arena."

"Is that going to be a problem?"

"Not at all. If anything goes wrong, it will be on her hands."

"I still don't like the way this is structured."

"They asked for a purge. They'll have one."

"Targets?"

The chairman sat down at the head of the table.

"Leave that to me."

Talbot got up and left the room.

He made his way to the lone office located in the lower level designated for him at the start of the operation to ensure privacy. As he entered the lift to take him down, he thought about Neil Shannon. Arrogant, strong, yet naïve. A man too full of himself to understand when he may be in over his head. The doors opened on to an empty corridor that led to a single door at the end. He walked down and swiped his wrist against the square panel on the side.

His office was sparsely furnished with a desk, chair and sofa. The windows had blinds that were closed shut, giving the space an eerie grey glow. He sat at the glass desk and swiped his hand across the surface. A holoscreen appeared on the wall before him displaying multiple files opened for viewing. His fingers maneuvered across the virtual keyboard as he typed in a code. The screen changed to a messenger page.

New plan. He typed.

Purge aborted? Was the reply.

No. New Purge stage added.

Implementation?

Upon completion of authorized transfer.

Details?

Will send them shortly.

Noted.

The screen went blank and he brought the files back up. He leaned back in his chair and began tugging his bottom lip. What he planned to do would cripple the economy in most of the American regions.

A dish best served cold.

His mouth curved into a spiteful grin.

With everyone involved in the operation seated and ready to start, the chairman called the meeting to order. The whiteness of the room felt stifling despite its openness. Early afternoon sunlight flooded the space, giving it an almost heavenly glow. A perfect effect for the righteous endeavor they were about to begin.

"Shall we get down to the business at hand?"

He took his place in the end seat.

"First step is infiltration, as we discussed. This will be for access to the networks and overall scouting of the region," his chief analyst stated.

"Next will be surveillance of the targets. We have to

be absolutely sure before proceeding with executing the plan," Talbot finished.

"That sounds good. I don't want any unnecessary bloodshed on our hands," his secretary added

"Bloodshed?" The scientist scoffed. "That should be the least of our worries considering."

The room went quiet in acknowledgement.

"So, how will the assignments be dispersed?" The chairman asked the telepath.

In a dark navy suit, the telepath looked like an agent of death. The light turned his eyes into glowing orbs. He had no expression. A cold darkness emitted from him.

"Twenty-five operatives for surveillance, fifteen agents collecting data and a four-man team to access the code sequence."

"Those are very specific numbers," the secretary said. He eyed the telepath suspiciously.

"You'll know why when it starts to go into full swing."

"What about the government agents?" The chairman asked.

"There are about a handful, as far as I can tell. They seem to be only working as watchers for the Organization. It's quite comical. Same goes for the Shadowmen. They have a few being deployed. One is even so far up the chain as to be involved with the U.S. Cabinet."

"Well, that will chafe the President if it ever comes out," one of the head scientists laughed.

"We propose a one-year timeline. That way the toll won't be so great on the rest of the residents not involved."

"The aftermath alone would be devastating."

The chairman steepled his hands.

"What is plan B?" The secretary leaned back in his chair and eyed everyone.

"In regard to what?" the lab tech asked.

"Contingency plan for if this all goes to hell and we are all exposed," he snapped.

The telepath undid his jacket and sat straight with his legs slightly apart

"When that happens, we will deal with it. But, the mission still stands. Once the agents activate the code, we move forward."

"If they can," the secretary blurted.

"No. I will send a second tier if necessary."

There were loud sharp intakes of breath around the table. Some looked to the chairman who stared back knowingly. He had conversed with Professor Bartley over the matter weeks ago and that was the consensus they came up with. Failure was not an option.

"Then it's settled." The chairman arose from his seat. "Let the new era of Bi-Genetic equality commence."

He saw the doubt in their faces along with a deep determination to see it through.

⤺

President Lynmore rocked in her chair as she stared out of the Oval Office window. On her desk lay a hard copy of the Shadow organizations plans for a purge. The information cost lives to get and was slipped in with the daily progress reports. With minimal input on what it entailed, she got the idea. By using the term purge, it conveyed a last resort. George, her Secretary of Homeland Security lounged on the sofa waiting for her to comment. She sat up straight, stopping the chair, and stared at him. He let out a loud sigh.

"Madame President, I don't need to tell you how dire this situation may turn out to be."

"What would you have me do then?" She snapped.

"Make sure we have our own people positioned

inside," he moved his arms in circular motions, "whatever this operation is."

"It sounds like a killing squad."

"Then, it probably is."

"I can't sanction the assassination of civilians!" She said sharply.

"It won't be our men doing it."

She pursed her lips in defiance and watched him lean forward in exasperation. His arms hung between his long legs and he turned his head to look at her.

"I want to know the targets and why. If we can remedy this without bloodshed…" She didn't finish.

"And when we find out?"

"I want a team dispatched to that monolith for oversight of the," she waved a limp hand, "Grid city."

"Done."

Perplexed, she opened her hands palms up on the desk.

"We haven't got the list yet."

George stood.

"Doesn't matter. We go in hot and make sure they know we mean business."

"I want this to be discreet," she admonished him.

"Absolutely." His expression said otherwise

He opened the door and stared down the secret service agent standing in his path. The man moved out of the way and positioned himself to the side of the frame. The way he avoided eye contact told the George what he suspected all along. Out of the corner of his eye as he walked down the hall, he saw the agent give a quick glance towards him.

Goddamn spies! He sneered in his head.

⌒

A holy mess is what came to Hana's mind as he went through the classified requisitions. Not only had the facility dispatched agents, but also Shannon and President Lynmore. There were too many hands in the pot and he knew it would blow up in all their faces. Given the fact that the Grid Community's existence had been exposed, the only choice left was for Hana to allow the government limited access. They requested full control and Hana made sure the President understood this was not her house. It was Shadow territory.

The commlink on his desk beeped.

"Sorry to bother you, sir." There was always that pause before saying sir.

"What is it?"

"General Perrara is on the secure line."

"Which one?"

"I'm sorry, sir?"

"Which General Perrara?" Hana pinched his nose.

"Oh. The younger."

"Thank you."

Hana tapped the blinking icon on his holoscreen and selected audio only.

"General, what can I do for you?"

"Are you that worn down to not speak face to face?"

"I just don't feel like having to look someone in the eye when I tell a lie."

"Doing a lot of that?"

"General," Hana said.

He could hear the soft tapping of a pen on the other end. The General did that when he was agitated.

"I want you to stay out of this purge operation," Perrara finally said.

"It's too late for that."

"No. It sounds like a bloodbath in the works. Take your family and get the hell out the city."

"You didn't need to tell me that. Where do you think I am right now?"

There was a long pause. Neither spoke. Hana knew what he was going to say.

"Good. I'm glad. I really wanted it to work, you know."

"So did I." Hana slouched in his chair.

The line went dead, disconnecting the call.

Humans just weren't ready.

EXECUTION STYLE

November 16 1:47pm

Childs shook with anticipation as he eased through the townhouse's first-floor window near the rear. He could feel tiny beads of sweat start to surface on his entire body, making his clothes stick to his flesh. The mission was a familiar one. He didn't understand why he was so tense. It finally occurred to him that he was after a young man he had been stalking the past six months who at the tender age of nineteen fueled Childs's hunger for ripe, soft male flesh. Being stealthy had its advantages. As far as Childs could tell the young man never noticed.

He was on the verge of imagining the act of love-making with the young man when a tick of a clock sent a jolt into the pit of his stomach. His body went rigid and his muscles locked in place, paralyzing him for just a moment. Trying to compose himself once more, he inhaled deep, let it out slowly, and then proceeded up the staircase leading to the master bedroom.

Still stiff from the surprise, he took his time. Childs knew that panic only lead to disaster and, of course, that was not a professional attitude. Getting the job done was all he cared about. Throughout his profession he was known to do that. He fantasized the young succulent creature upstairs calling to him.

Reaching the bedroom door, he opened it and found his subject lying face down on the bed with one arm dangling over the side. Dark hair splayed across the pillows and down past the young man's shoulders. Pink full lips were parted slightly with soft snoring sounds escaping from them. Childs shut the door and crept silently across the room to climb onto the bed. While unzipping his jacket, he ran his fingers through the young man's hair, feeling the softness of it. He took his jacket off slowly, taking hold of the syringe he had extracted from the inside breast pocket. Feeling movement, the young man's eyes fluttered open and he turned.

November 17 5:16am

Sgt. Christopher Landers shook his head in disgust at the body on the stretcher as his stomach lurched. It was too early in the morning for his tastes and to see carnage like that after just waking up was too much. Even the sun had not attempted to peek out yet. Yellow tape was being spun across the crime scene as neighbors, awakened from deep sleep by the flashing red and blue lights, opened their front doors to witness the aftermath. He turned away from the house previous resided by the victim and walked over to his partner of five years.

"Looks the same as the others, doesn't it?" Landers said, nodding his head towards the corpse being loaded into the coroner van.

Thomas Munston was a big man compared to most. Standing at six feet four inches, he had Landers by three inches and where Landers was lean muscle, Munston was built like a football player; all brawn. His dark brown hair was cut short and well groomed. He was always clean shaven and smelled of aftershave. Eyes the color of stormy blue waters had seen too much in their lives.

"This one ain't so bad. The other one was mutilated."

He frowned at his own nonchalant response.

"Any patterns or records so far? I know the team is working hard on it."

"Nope, nothing, and that's what bothers me."

Munston surveyed the area one last time searching for tiny clues.

"There has to be something." Landers ran a hand through his dirty blonde hair and sighed. The doors of the coroner's van slammed shut and the meat wagon proceeded down the street.

"Yeah, maybe. We may never know, huh?"

"Damn, damn, damn! I hate cases like these."

"It's not the end of the world, Landers. Come on, we got some other leads to comb through."

"Oh, really? Where?"

"Just, come on! What have we got to lose?"

The two detectives headed to the unmarked sedan they rode up in and got in, Landers in the driver's seat. Breakfast would have to be now or never even though they felt it too early in the morning. It was going to be a long day.

10:04 p.m.

Dowans checked the window for the lock and finding it, used a laser cutter to make a small rectangular opening. He inserted a finger to flick it over and opened the window, climbing through. Inside, the watch dog was sleeping peacefully, oblivious to the intruder. Worthless. Dowans bent down and opened his bag consisting of syringes, chemicals, drugs and weapons. Filling one syringe with a powerful animal tranquilizer he injected it into the beast for good measure. He didn't like surprises, or dogs. Next, he proceeded to the bedroom upstairs.

Footsteps sounded on the carpeted stairs and Dowans ran behind a nearby wall to hide. A young woman in a long nightgown went into the kitchen and opened the refrigerator. She pulled out a container of juice and poured some in a glass. Heading back up the stairs to her room, she didn't notice Dowans silently stalking behind her. Going in, unaware he crept in a quarter of a second after, she shut the door.

Dowans leaned against the wall and took a deep breath because his eagerness was too intense. After killing her, he could go home and watch the boxing match on pay per view. He stood staring at her for what seemed like eternity. The girl still hadn't seen him.

She sat on her bed and swinging her legs up to lie down, she finally did. She sucked in her breath and reached for the lamp.

"Come any closer and I'll beat the shit out of you with this."

Her voice was shaky yet firm in tone. Amused, Dowans advanced on her in one leap as she swung. The lamp caught him in the temple. She used two fingers to try and poke him in the eyes. Not deterred, he leaned sideways and grabbed hold of them, snapping the fingers back. She screamed for a split second and brought her knee up, hitting him in the chest.

This one is going to be a fighter, he laughed silently. He had been in many fights and she was giving him a decent run for his money.

Good. Makes me want to off her even more.

11:15 p.m.

Emerson noticed the fear in the boy's eyes as he backed up against a wall. He had screwed up step one and now had to race time to catch his prey off guard. The boy opened the basement door and descended into darkness. He slowly followed. The little brat had been real mouthy earlier talking about how Emerson was going to pay for breaking into his house due to who is father was.

His father was exactly the reason why he came.

Shaw, the assistant city manager, was a corrupt politician whose entire immediately family members, said brat included, engaged in administering horrors to the poor and downtrodden. Their specialty was abandoned Bi-Genetics living on their own in the streets. Emerson's mission tonight involved sending a message to the manager and releasing his own brand of hell on them.

The basement was huge and maze like, though not difficult since he was used to unlit places. Infrared goggles he had picked up some years back were a handy tool, especially in this situation, since starting the sequence. He used them to track the Shaw brat and found him hiding in a room built into the far wall approximately four feet high. Without wasting time, Emerson grabbed him. The boy tried to squirm away, so he slammed his body into the floor. As he sought balance to raise himself up, Emerson punched him in the side of the head. His victim slid unconscious to the floor. Now, he could move on to step three.

November 22 4:07a.m.

Landers peeked at the body then turned away to vomit. Munston stood shaking his head. The body was mutilated and found wrapped in plastic, weighed down in the swimming pool. Her remains were practically drained of blood. Both detectives seemed to be getting pissed off with the investigation.

"This is the fourth one and we still don't have a clue." Landers used a napkin given to him by another officer to wipe his mouth.

"Never said it was going to be easy."

Munston pinched his nose between the eyes.

"Let's try that locked file we found last week. The one our people couldn't get access to. I know a really good hacker."

"Can't."

"What do you mean, can't?"

"It's not at the department anymore."

"What?" Landers yelled, forgetting he was at a crime scene.

"Look," Munston rubbed his eyes then turned to his partner. "We need a break, I get that. We also need to rest. Get some sleep."

"These people are getting killed by professional monsters! Maniacs!"

"I know, but we're wearing ourselves out."

"I didn't expect this attitude from you."

Landers cocked his head to one side.

"I'm not the one who stays at the station overnight working on this case. Why are you doing all that?"

"Because," Landers turned away, heading for the car, "it scares me to death."

Landers got home and went directly to the fridge. He threw his jacket beside him as he sat down on the sofa with a can of beer. Exhausted, he relished in the few moments of peace. Before he could crack open his brew, the phone rang. Another body had been found and Munston wanted him to come down to the crime scene. Exhaling loudly, he heaved himself off the couch, donned his jacket and raced out the door to his car. The murders were happening too close together. He was starting to hate his job.

10:27 p.m.

Felps drummed his fingers on the steering wheel as he waited for the young man to get out of the car. The man named Jeff slammed the door shut and walked up the stairs to his aunt's apartment. Felps got out of his car and into the man's back seat where he would wait until the guy came back. He checked his watch. It would take twenty minutes to get to Jeff's house meaning he would wait five minutes then move on him. Five more minutes to do the job and then it was back to deep freeze for a long nap.

He hated being out in society longer than a few months. As part of his job, due diligence was required for surveillance of the targets before executing the plan. His prey this time was a rich, up and coming business owner who happened to dabble in human trafficking of Bi-Genetics for sex trade purposes. Felps had infiltrated one of the office buildings as a high rolling client and couldn't believe the operation going on within the top floors. Some of the things being done to the workers by paying clients made his insides burn with rage. Getting rid of Mr. Jeffrey would be his pleasure.

Jeff came out of the building smiling and went to his car. Felps knew he had just spun a web of lies to his Aunt about his dedication to various charities since she was on the board of many. He watched Jeff get in the car, push the ignition button and head towards home. Five minutes later, the car stopped in the middle of the road with music blasting from it.

The struggle had begun.

⌒

Brian blended into the environment easily. Wearing a polo shirt, Bermuda shorts and a baseball cap, his appearance resembled other young men in the library. He carried nothing in his hands. Surveying the section of tables, he spotted his target getting up to return a book on its shelf. He slipped a small chip encased in hard, plastic tube from his shorts' pocket into her tablet's protective sleeve laying on the table before she got back. While leaving, he turned to see her pick up her things, the college lanyard swinging wide, as she headed out. He grinned.

Quelly sat down at her terminal in the small studio apartment she rented and pulled out her tablet. The hard tube rolled out from the sleeve, making her frown. She swore it had been in her backpack. Being tired from mid-terms, it was possible she made a mistake. She inserted the memory chip into the designated slot on her monitor and typed in her code. Nothing happened. A second try resulted in the same blank screen. Her tanned complexion and tight dark curls reflected on it as she stared, confused.

With her hands clenched on the sides of the desk she looked down and noticed a bar blinking on the bottom corner of the screen with a word slightly visible behind. As a science major, she had some hacking skills so after the fourth attempt to remove the bar, she was successful and saw what appeared to be the password. Typing it in, a menu popped up and she gasped. This was definitely not her memory chip after all, meaning one thing; she had been activated.

The Shadow Organization had recruited her so long ago that after waiting years for a call she put it aside and focused on her studies. Her stint with the ROTC in high school by way of waiver from her parents due to her age caught their eye. She was all of thirteen years old as a sophomore and a registered scientific genius. By the time her four-year college term was up, she had been in training camps with top scientists to take part in advance technologies. Now, at twenty, working on her doctorate, she was finally allowed to have some fun as a Shadow agent.

What the mission entailed did not faze her. The world had become a cruel and vicious place with misguided souls not able to see the big picture. She shook her head in disappointment for humanity while she scrolled through the files populating the screen in rapid succession. There would be a short window for learning the ins and outs of the system.

One file entry named Sequence Surveillance looked interesting. She opened it and a list of names in alphabetical order with codes along with locations next to them were displayed. Information regarding where video footage would be located was also attached.

Hard copy?

That was rare considering cloud-based data storage was currently the norm. She wrote down the address of the first one and abandoning her studies for the evening, went for a drive to get it. Her tablet sat on the passenger seat as a precaution in case it was necessary. For all she knew, the data could be old school cartridges or microfiche. That made her smile a bit. Another frown creased her face the entire drive.

It's begun.

10:20 p.m.

Through the house's front bay window, Garrison watched the young woman go into the living room. He jumped down from the tree he was hiding in, landing with minimal noise, and headed towards the side. This was his thirteenth mission for his unknown employer.

There were hints as to whomever they might be. He made it a point to never ask those questions. As long as he got paid and not caught, the rest was moot. Over the last four years the jobs had become a bore simply because they were too easy. All he wanted to do now was kill the person then do as he pleased to them afterwards. Murder was a fine art that should be enjoyed. Not a click, a bang, and a thank you ma'am. The kill was even better if the target had evil in them.

Proceeding into the house via an open window, he watched every corner of the nosy neighborhood. Because everyone appeared to look out for each other, doors and windows were hardly ever secured. He shook his head in disappointment. Trust no one. Especially when you're part of something sinister like most of the people in that sector. Inside, he saw her head for the kitchen. He didn't follow. There were too many utensils she could use to defend herself. In the living room, he sat down on the sofa facing the stairway and observed the dark, spacious room perfect for a crime. Garrison made himself comfortable.

She came out of the kitchen and sat on the sofa opposite him, holding a pint of ice cream. As she was about to dig in with the large spoon, she saw him sitting, waiting. She set the ice cream down on the coffee table and laying the spoon next to it, didn't move. There they sat looking at each other.

"Is that strawberry?" Garrison broke the silence. She looked down at the pint and nodded. "You don't mind, do you?" He pointed as she shook her head. Picking up the pint and spoon, he shoved a few bites in his mouth. After a few minutes, she spoke.

"Who are you?"

Garrison looked at her and smiled. He could tell by how at ease and unafraid she was that he was going to enjoy himself by far. The young woman had done horrible things to adults who defended Bi-Genetics. There would be no show of mercy. Evil oozed from her very being.

"What do you think?"

"A burglar, murderer, rapist, whatever."

Her eyes had the malice of someone who ruined lives for fun, which she did often.

"All of the above." He watched her eyes narrow. "Before I get on with it, are you going to be cooperative and go quietly? Or, do I have to chase you and get very rude and nasty?" She scrambled off the couch and bolted for the kitchen. "A struggle it is then."

He stood and went after her before she could reach its threshold. Her expertise with knives was not something he relished to experience firsthand.

November 27

Munston walked away from the scene in disgust. What seemed like a car wreck on the outskirts of the neighborhood turned out to be another murder. At first the detective thought the gas tank had blown. Closer scrutiny revealed the flames came from inside the vehicle. The body was trapped in the car that had to have been pushed into the thousand feet deep ravine. Although the body was charred beyond recognition, there was no mistaking the vehicle, and everyone knew the owner didn't let anyone else drive it. He had lost count of how many prominent community figures or their children were ending up in the morgue. Munston headed to the station to file his report.

Thanksgiving was officially ruined.

While driving through the parking lot towards the station, he saw a man wearing all black go into the research laboratory the next building over. Being curious, since no one just walked in unless you were authorized, and this guy didn't look it, Munston parked his car in the lot and went up to a nearby security guard.

"Excuse me. I'm Detective Munston, homicide." He flashed his badge. "I'd like to know who that man was just walked in."

"Oh, that's one of our computer analysts, sir. He comes in every few days."

"Thank you, officer."

Munston decided to take a chance and went straight after the man, following him all the way into a computer lab. Whenever someone attempted to question him, he flashed his badge and kept on moving. At a corridor ahead, the man turned into an office with floor to ceiling windows. The bright sun made the room glow. He was about to introduce himself when the man whipped around and yelled.

"What did you fuck up this time?" The deep frown on his face dropped as he realized Munston was not who he expected. "I'm sorry, I thought you were my assistant. May I help you?"

He was now puzzled by the intrusion and Munston took it as his cue.

Again, he pulled out his badge and showed it to the man. As the man looked at the badge and him to compare, Munston saw how young the man looked. His skin was flawless, not quite pale and his eyes seemed to slightly glint. Dark brown hair cut short was styled like many of the college aged men around the city. Nothing unusual, yet…

"You looked kind of peculiar walking in here with that on." He nodded at the dark casual outfit. "Not wearing a lab coat today?"

"I don't need a lab coat to type on a computer. You are referring to the forensics people on the fifth floor." The man's tone was deadpan.

"Oh." Munston went over to the main terminal and tapped on the cube shaped mini tower. "So, what do you type into this baby's mem?" It was a state of the art touch enabled computer system.

The young man sighed and sat down at his desk. He swiped his arm across the top and a virtual keyboard appeared. Typing in his passcode a 3-D hologram of community sixteen came up. Every person and their statistics were listed on a panel near the bottom right corner.

"I keep record of everyone in the city, including new entries. We can't have anomalies in the registry." He swung around to face Munston. "Does that answer any of your queries?" He rubbed under his nose and sniffed.

Munston, feeling a bit idiotic, nodded and said, "Yes. Yes, it does. I am truly sorry for intruding. Thanks." He stopped at the door and looked back. "How old are you, anyway?"

The man gave a hollow laugh. "Twenty-four." Then went back to his work, already oblivious to his guest.

Munston got back into his car and banged his head on the steering wheel. Something about that analyst disturbed him but he couldn't put his finger on it. The way his eyes seemed to be void of everything creeped him out. He almost drove off before remembering he had to file his report at the station. In his office, his mind kept going over the analyst and the information he controlled. Something didn't sit right with him.

Brian frowned as Munston's presence lingered long after being gone. He not only hated regular humans but hated nosy ones more than anything. The murders were coming hard and fast and he understood law enforcements frustration. None of it mattered to him. In his mind, there was no sympathy for any of the victims.

From the distance between his office and the parking lot, he could hear the detective's thoughts resonate like an echo chamber.

You're correct, human.

He let out a soft laugh. To deem himself as the same species went out the window long ago. One couldn't deny their true nature once reality set in. Pushing that out of his mind, he went back to the task interrupted. His long pale fingers typed in the access code to Quelly's computer from his remote terminal and retrieved the information he needed. Hers was to remain open during specific times for transfers.

He closed the file after the download, leaving no trace he had been there and opened it on his own. Community eleven was brought up on his screen. From the list attached, he selected one of the names for a new task. It was going to be a long day, and he didn't want to report to his employer for fear of what he might have to do when darkness fell.

9:15 pm

Coming to the abandoned train station, Hammond slowed his pursuit and began to stroll towards the open doors of a wrecked box car. The night air had a chill with no clouds in the sky. He could hear the heavy breathing of the frightened young man. In the beginning of the chase, Tommy was all bad ass and shit talk until he realized Hammond was not someone easily intimidated, if at all. He had tracked Tommy from an emergency meeting held by the community leaders after an affluent business owner was found dead.

Tommy was hiding between two seats in the coach section of a half-rusted rail car. He grabbed him by the neck, picking him off the floor and grinned. Tommy's eyes opened fully and as his mouth opened, Hammond used both hands to yank Tommy's head to one side with a loud crack. He really didn't want to waste his energy on scum like Tommy. Hammond dropped the body then took off his gloves. Quick and dirty. That's the way he liked his missions.

Serves you right, you evil fuck.

Hammond smirked, heading for a great Italian restaurant he had heard about.

Munston didn't care for seeing more bodies in such a short time span. The victim was a female in her mid-thirties, her body found half sunk in mud with earth worms crawling around inside the wounds. It was a gruesome sight, made worse by being called in from his lunch break. His half-digested lunch ejected from his mouth and spooled around the bush near the front porch as he tried to clear his head. He hated vomiting.

An investigator holding a tablet in his hand came up to him after the body was hauled off. He flipped the screen around to show a list and began to explain before Munston could even ask.

"Over the past few days, or weeks rather, a small amount of men were put in deep freeze. None of them had any injuries or wounds. Matter of fact, they just walked in to the facility and voila."

"So?" Munston was irritated. He wanted to rinse out his mouth.

"So, think about it. A few hours after each murder, some guy goes into deep freeze."

"Let me see that." Munston snatched the tablet from the investigator's hands and scanned it. "Have these times and dates been verified with our labs?" He looked at the list again.

Addams, Jeffrey	Nov. 7	5:16 a.m.
Brent, Cecil A.	Nov. 11	4:45 a.m.
Dowans, Raym	Nov. 17	11:34 p.m.
Emerson, Christ	Nov. 21	12:45 p.m.
Felps, Eric	Nov. 22	11:57 p.m.
Garrison, Andre	Nov. 25	11:50 p.m.
Hammond, Steve	Nov. 27	2:15 p.m.

As Munston read the names he commented, "These are in alphabetical order." The investigator nodded. "Wait! This last one is today's date." Both men concluded what that meant. "Oh, shit! There's a body lying around somewhere!"

"What a way to spend Thanksgiving."

The investigator shook his head.

Landers suddenly pulled up in his car and parked next to them. He approached the two men and was about to ask about the crime scene when Munston handed him the tablet. They explained while he perused the document, his complexion going pale.

"Look at the bottom one." Munston pointed on the paper. "Where's that body?"

Landers looked up at him and shook his head.

"You don't seem that surprised, Landers," Munston said.

"At this point, are you?" Landers replied as he did his own canvas around the crime scene. "There's not much else we can say about it."

He turned to give Munston a questioning stare as he nodded at the vomit laden bush.

"If you saw the body, you would have too."

"Hmm." Landers stood up and brushed off his pants. "So now what?"

"We go hunting for a body."

"Wanna' go get something to eat first?" Landers asked jokingly.

"That's not funny. Not funny at all."

As the attendants covered the missing victim's body, Munston breathed a sigh of relief. Now that he knew what was going on the case would be a little easier. The department was getting a warrant to release all the suspects from deep freeze for questioning. An officer handed him the identification card. Thomas Holt III. He knew the name of the Mayor's assistant. Another high profile killing. Munston got into his car and left with one thought on his mind. The person who broke that poor guy's neck was hella strong.

While he signed in at the station, he heard someone yelling his name from down the hall. He turned to see a fellow officer waving for him to hurry. Not seeing the need of importance, he reluctantly went to see what the fuss was all about.

"We got incoming. The killers are being transported here. We already have a man by the name of Christopher Emerson who was pulled out of deep freeze a little while ago." The officer blurted out. "Chief says he's to be questioned on the cellar murder. And keep it under wraps for now."

Munston remembered that murder and went green with sickness. He was about to meet a man who tore people apart for a living.

"Bring him into interrogation room four," Munston whispered.

The officer ran over to his counterpart and gave instructions out of ear shot. When the officer came back to Munston, the two men walked together, making sure no one followed out of curiosity. His superior along with two reps from the prosecutor's office and more officers stood on the other side of the two-way mirror. He entered the room and checked to make sure nothing was lying around then nodded at the officer standing guard outside.

A seemingly young man with chestnut curls and golden eyes was brought into the room. He was about six feet three inches tall and had an expression of boredom at being interrogated. Sitting down, he straddled the seat and kept perfect upright posture.

"Name?" Munston tried to sound bored too. He could hear the edge in his voice.

"I think you know that already."

The man's pitch was dead pan.

"Age?"

"Thirty-six years, three months."

"Very good. Why are you going around killing and mutilating people?"

"Because it's my job and I felt like it at the time."

Munston was taken aback. Everyone on the other side of the glass stared back in shock.

"You don't deny it?"

A full confession looked to be in the cards.

"Be lucky I screwed up." He leaned forward and locked eyes with Munston. "I could have done more than tear him apart."

"Did you use your bare hands?"

Munston cleared his throat.

"I had on gloves, but yes."

"Pretty strong guy, huh?" Munston looked down on the report and saw a colleague of Emerson's on it. "Know a guy name Ray Dowans?" Emerson grinned. "Well?"

"No," Emerson spat out, his eyes narrowing.

As he spoke those magic words, an officer outside called to the guard, "Bring in the other one!"

Dowans was led into the room along with another chair and seated next to Emerson.

"They woke you up, too? Man, we're gonna' get fried

now, huh?" Dowans chuckled.

"I thought you didn't know him?" Munston was smirking now.

"You're not going to save your own ass and leave me stranded here, my good buddy."

Dowans was having a good time rubbing Emerson the wrong way laughing until he turned and saw the glare Emerson gave him.

"Ray." Munston continued his questioning with him. "Did you also kill your victim with your bare hands?"

"No, she died of penile penetration." His blue eyes sparkled wit amusement.

"Don't be a wise ass!"

Munston slammed his fists on the table.

Another glare from Emerson made Dowans straighten his posture and answer. He cleared his throat and responded.

"Yes, I did." He turned to Emerson. "Happy now?"

"Very." Through gritted teeth came the reply.

Munston was perplexed. Why the confession? Was Emerson the ring leader? Why did Dowans seem to fear him? He glanced over at the mirror and begged for assistance with a stare. All the questions he wanted to ask fled from his head. As if noticing this, Emerson leaned forward.

"Speechless? I'll grant you that. But you haven't asked the right ones yet. And this whole confession thing." Emerson sat back with a wide grin. "I was totally joking. I figured it was what you all wanted to hear. Oh, and we need a lawyer."

An officer came in with one cup of water. Emerson smirked at the obvious tactic. Munston realized he was in over his head with the investigation. The entire interview was being recorded and Emerson knew it. He essentially tanked everything said within the last few minutes.

By late the next morning all the previously frozen suspects were assembled in the precinct's conference room turned interrogation space under strict gag orders. No one was allowed to leak any information regarding the case to the media. What baffled everyone was the fact that none of the suspects denied doing the crimes despite their requests for legal representation being stalled. Munston found that alone peculiar. He needed to find their purpose. Getting an answer terrified him.

"Name?" He asked the first man on the end. This time Munston was not trying to be nice.

"Jeff Addams," the man with long brown hair answered. "Yours?"

"All he wanted was your name, not a wise crack."

The man to his right shot him a look of pure hatred. Addams didn't flinch, meeting his gaze.

"Age?"

"Twenty-five. Is there any water around here? I'm parched."

"You're going to be punched in a minute." The other man warned him.

Munston turned to the agitated man. "Name?"

"Andrew Joseph Garrison. Age twenty-six."

"Is that like your full name?"

One of the other suspects asked, giggling.

Garrison's eyes become hot pools of flames, brown turning to cinnamon.

"Who's your employer?"

"Is that important?" Emerson interjected.

"Yes, it is. Who is it?"

"No idea." Addams said.

"Excuse me?" Munston was incredulous.

"We don't know. We just get an assignment and do it." Garrison shrugged.

"Not one of you know?"

"No," a few answered together.

Munston cleared his throat again and took another glance at the deep freeze list.

"There is one person not on this list who, according to the facility technicians, should be. His name is Eugene Childs."

Garrison's face took on a confused expression. He looked towards Hammond and they seemed to exchange communication in silence. Munston got the impression that it was not like Childs to disobey orders. Finally, Hammond spoke up.

"Three guesses. Either something went wrong, Childs hid the body too well, or the victim is still alive and Childs is with him. He has a thing for the young boys."

Landers had entered the room and stood in the corner by the door.

"When you say a thing…" Munston stopped as the room went silent.

By the look on his face he immediately began to feel ill.

"Where did this take place, the," Munston licked his lips dried up from talking most of the day, "assignment?"

"In the twenty seventh grid district." Felps tapped his lower lip. "I think the kid's name was Kyle. That's all I know."

"Oh, I think you know more than that," Munston said under his breath as he motioned for the guard. He whispered for him to get an investigator to check it out. He noticed Landers not smiling. Both were worried something awful or unprecedented was about to drop. Not too soon, but it was coming.

⌣

December 1

Why did it have to be a rainy day? Ilan asked himself while picking the lock on the front door.

He blew a few strands of his dark red hair that somehow unwound themselves, out of the tight ponytail, from his face. Hearing a click, he advanced into the house only to knock over a ceramic lamp that he was not aware of.

When did that get there?

He had scoped the house two days before and there were no indications of the people living there remodeling. Moments later a deep voice came from the stairway.

"Who's there?"

"What's going on?" A female voice whispered.

Ilan froze with pure anxiety and stayed that way even as the man and woman came down the stairs. For a split second the two men locked eyes.

"The fuck…!" Was all the man got out before he jumped Ilan.

His fists slammed into Ilan repeatedly, barely giving him enough time to block the blows. Ilan finally found an opening and turned the tables by bringing his knee up with full force, knocking the guy back. The fight was getting too ferocious for his tastes when the woman finally grabbed a decorative piece from the mantel and hit Ilan in the back of the head as he sat atop the guy delivering punches. He fell sideways to the floor and didn't move for a brief second in surprise.

When the man came into visual range, Ilan turned over and kicked him hard in the chest. The man went flying into the wall used for hanging coats and one of the wooden pegs embedded itself into the back of his head. His eyes rolled up in their sockets and the body's weight forced the peg out of the wall as he fell face down.

The woman screamed. Ilan threw a large glass figurine as she opened her mouth for a second wind, hitting her exposed teeth. Shattered pieces slid down her throat. Her eyes bulged. With hands gripping her neck she hunched over and began pacing. After a few ragged gargles she also hit the floor face down. Her body convulsed for what seemed like minutes. It didn't take her long to die when she stopped.

"Shit, shit, shit!"

Ilan plopped down on the couch with his head in his hands. He reached into his pocket and pulled out an old school smart phone. Dialing Garrison's number, he typed a message then went to deal with the bodies.

Garrison's personal handler had infiltrated the precinct and showed up at the holding cell to hand him a commlink ear piece. The man turned away and stood a few feet from the bars to make sure no one came to disturb him or ask too many questions. Garrison whispered his code word and heard it connect to his answering service. He listened to his messages then came to the last one, hearing the automated female voice calmly convey Ilan's frantic text.

"I think I screwed up. Some guy was there and jumped me. I didn't know what to do so I killed both of them. I gotta' straighten it out at headquarters."

Disconnecting, he went back to the bars and slipped it into the handler's hand. It was pocketed quickly before he opened the cell to escort him and the rest of the group to the interrogation room. While the suspects were left alone in the room, he relayed Ilan's dilemma in a soft whisper. Security had been lax the past few hours and no one was listening on the other side of the two way.

"I knew he was gonna' screw this up," Dowans stated.

"It wasn't his fault. Someone else was there besides

the woman. I would have done the same thing," Emerson interjected.

"Anyway," Garrison continued, "he has to fix it. I hope he makes sure no one is following him." He got up and looked towards the opened slat window near the ceiling that brought in air from outside. Only a part of the city could be seen in the night sky. He knew it was all lit up and beautiful as ever. Somewhere out there among the city lights two bodies lay on the floor in one of those houses. He felt accomplished somehow.

"When can we get out of here?" Hammond asked impatiently.

"We have connections. Be calm." Brent assured him. "It won't be long."

"I want to go home and have a real meal for a change."

"Who doesn't?" Garrison snapped.

CHAPTER THREE

CHANGE OF PLANS

Jansen went up the walkway of the third house in the prestigious neighborhood and knocked on the front door. It was mid-morning and most of the residents were gone for work or socializing. He wore a polo shirt and khakis. The clipboard in his hand had a local network company logo. Through the window, he could see movement then door swung open.

A young man stood red faced in a pair of boxers and a robe. His hands clenched into fists.

"What the shit, man? I called like two hours ago for you fuck heads to come and fix my internet. I got shit to do!"

With each onslaught of profanity, Jansen began to like him even less.

"Sorry, man. Traffic."

"Whatever. It's in the back." The man moved out of the way to let him pass. "And don't touch anything else," he yelled over his shoulder as he walked away.

In the back office was a forest of plants with a large glass desk in the center. The double monitors were frozen in the middle of a live stream. As he knelt to check the wiring, he glanced up at the images. His eyes went wide in horror then slanted in disgust.

"Hey, how long is this gonna' take?" The young man had come in without Jansen noticing.

"Oh, not long."

119

Jansen stood and grabbed the guy by the neck, slamming him down into the desk. It cracked, forming a web. When he let go, to his surprise, the young man got hold of his legs and brought him to the floor. Momentarily dazed, Jansen watched the guy leap over him and bolt further into the house.

"Well, then. I guess we're going for a fight today," he muttered to himself.

Within minutes, he found the guy in the back den trying to get the into his father's gun rack. Jansen came up on him fast and hand chopped him in the shoulder. The kid yelled out from the pain and before Jansen could finish, he scuttled off into the next room.

The room was dark inside and Jansen had to force his eyes to adjust. He scanned the room, listening for the faint sound of breathing and went towards that direction.

"You're pathetic, you know that?" The young man was hunched in a corner with Jansen kneeling in front of him. "Do you want to die?" The man shook his head. "I didn't hear you." Jansen leveled the gun, silencer already attached.

"No, please! I don't want to die!"

Snot ran down his face.

"Say it again."

"Please!" The kid tried to get up, but his legs were too weak from fear.

Jansen smiled and stood over him.

"I don't believe you. How many begged for help or mercy and you denied them? You had so much fun, but I see you can't take what you dish out."

"Please, I have lots of money! I can get you anyone you want!"

He shot him twice; once in the head and another in the heart. Blood spatter covered the wall behind the slumped body.

Pleased with his work, Jansen left the house to head home. On the way out, he passed the computer room and took another look at the screens. He wished he had made the kid suffer more for what he had been doing to Bi-Genetics. The sequence had changed so deep freeze was no longer a viable option. He shut the front door and walked the three blocks back to his car.

~

Landers sat at his office desk pondering over where Childs could be. It was the sixth of December and no one had yet sighted him or Kyle. After a while, he started to worry. Munston came bursting in, full of rage, scaring him out of his reverie. The man paced the floor for a moment then pounded his fists on Landers' desk.

"Why?" He hollered, searching Landers' face. "That's all I want to know!"

"What are you talking about?"

Landers sat up puzzled by his question.

"You went against our emergency procedures and had bail set for three of those fucking murderers!"

"Because we had no definite proof that they killed anybody, and they have the right to due process before we interrogate them any further."

"They confessed!"

"For all we know, this is a set up and they are a bunch of nut jobs and liars."

Munston reached to draw his weapon and appeared ready to shoot him when an officer came in to report another body. He fled out of the office, swearing profusely. Landers got up slowly. He had no desire to gather up more information on these murders. Besides, it was almost over.

The body was buried in the backyard along with another. The woman's neck was split open from the inside.

A purple line from her neck down to her abdomen bulged upward. A coroner took his scalpel and cut through a small section of the line. Green glass could be seen under the skin, which caused detectives Landers and Munston to turn equal in color. They went their separate ways to regain their composure.

Coming back to the body, Landers instinctively wiped his already dry mouth and coughed. "Someone pretty sick in the head made her eat glass like that."

"Cover it up!" Munston commanded the coroner, through grimacing.

Killian knew by the pain in his chest it was going to be a rough day. Christmas was coming soon, and he wanted to be at home, not in a body bag or hiding out in a shed or something. He also knew the young nineteen-year-old girl named Lisa was alone in her bedroom. No one at the party even knew she had went upstairs.

The party had scenes resembling something out of Caligula: the worse ones. Lisa helped her sugar daddy pick out and buy young males and females for the explicit use of public sexual depravity. If you had the entry door fee of 10,000 credits and were on the membership list, loads of entertainment awaited you. Designated rooms in the back of the estate were soundproofed so neighbors would not hear the screams. It took all of Killian's mental strength to keep his sanity and remain calm.

He stood in the middle of the hallway outside her door pondering over what to do when some privileged slut wearing too much makeup, and obviously drunk, came drooling towards him. As she went for a lunge, Killian dodged, slithering past her and into Lisa's room.

Lisa was sitting on her bed with a pained expression on her face. She turned to Killian and screamed at him,

"What are you doing in here? Get out! I don't want

to talk to anyone!" Then she broke down and cried, tears fast streaming along with snot running from her nose.

Killian decided to play the role of comforter. He sat down on the bed beside her and gave her a hug. Just being near her, let alone touching her, made his skin crawl and he felt nauseous. Her skinny shoulders held a head full of big curls too heavy for them. She reminded him of those bobble head figures from the early 21st century.

"I wish I were dead," she sniffed, wiping snot and tears from her face.

"It may be sooner than you think," Killian laughed.

"Wha…"

Killian quickly grabbed the pillow from behind her and pushed it into her face, sending her down onto the bed struggling for air. He patiently waited until her body ceased moving and then a few minutes more for good measure to make sure she was dead. Tucking the pillow under her head, he left through the window. She got a better death than she deserved.

"That was easy." Killian deeply inhaled the night air and exhaled slowly. "Now, for the real fun."

He went to the rear of the estate and snuck back in. The screams no one from the outside could hear came not from excitement. He delivered fear and death with swift efficiency. When he completed his mission twenty minutes later, a feeling of hunger struck him. He headed for the valet post to retrieve his car. There was a good Italian place not far from his location.

Landers sat at home watching the daily news with disinterest when his telecom rang. Its blue light flashed frantically. He tapped the connect icon and listened to a hysterical man on the other end request to meet immediately. Sighing, Landers went down to his car and got in. It occurred to him what day it was, and he thought maybe something had gone wrong, cancelling his mission. He could only hope.

The meeting place was fifty miles from his apartment, on the outskirts of the city and secluded. He turned on a hidden road per the instructions to cover his trail and not be traced. Parking his car in front of the only giant willow tree, he saw a squirrel scurry up the branches while he waited. He found it hard to believe how much he still loved nature since at this point his concern for human life turned sour. He felt the two should somehow coexist.

Another car pulled up and a young man got out. Landers knew who he was at once. Jeremiah Winters gave the impression that he definitely had no regard for human life. Even in the dark of night, Winters' grey eyes nearly glowed like some unholy messenger. The two men shook hands then crossed the road into the nature park.

"We have to remove Childs from the database and all the memory banks." Winters started. "Every government agency and all the other bozos are after him. See the problem?"

Landers frowned, nodding in agreement.

"Make it so he doesn't exist except in someone's imagination." He saw Winters nod. "I can erase his prints, birth certificate, and current information. Sound good?"

"Sounds great," Winters spat into the tall grass, his reply sounding like sarcasm. "Just remember, he needs to be kept hidden once he's found."

"One thing."

"Hmm?"

"What happened with Childs? It's been over month." Landers stopped walking.

"My assumption is he's hiding out with his victim, who is alive and kicking."

"Why would he keep the boy alive?" Right after he said, he knew the answer.

"We all have an idea, don't we?"

Winters halted and turned back to him.

"When should I get ready?"

"Soon. It should take place an hour past midnight." Winters headed back to his car, leaving Landers to his own thoughts.

Landers turned to walk back to his own car and stopped dead in his tracks. Someone was nearby, and it wasn't Winters. Hand on his gun, he crouched low, ready to take out whoever it was. A streak of blond moved in the distance.

Childs waited behind a large boulder further in the grass for Winters and Landers to finish their talk regarding him. The whole erasing of his data sounded good to him as well. Right now, he didn't care about that. He needed help first, for Kyle. Seeing Landers alone, he made his move and approached. He forgot Landers was carrying a gun and froze as the muzzle rose to point right between his eyes.

"Childs?" Landers whispered incredulous, looking around. "Is that you?"

"Please, you gotta' help me," Childs whispered back.

As he came into the dim light beaming from the park posts, he watched Landers search him from head to toe with his eyes. His dark tunic was stiff in places where blood had dried and red stained his fingers. His blond hair displayed thin lines of burgundy. He motioned for Landers to follow when he lowered his gun.

They walked at least a half mile before arriving at Childs' hiding place that turned out to be an old shed of sorts near a dried-up ravine. Going inside, the young Kyle lay on the floor nearly bleeding to death and in obvious pain.

"Why?" Landers asked staring down at the carnage.

"He wouldn't die so I thought, well," Childs became shy, "I should just keep him for myself." He looked Landers square in the eyes. "I wanna' help but I haven't been able to move him since yesterday. His wounds keep opening up."

"Jesus," Landers said softly, sinking down on the floor.

12:37 a.m.

Quelly sat down at the terminal and inserted the memory chip. She had received a lot of info on how to retrieve the video footage of the crimes and keep it from the people surrounding her. The sequence was clear, and must seem like a big joke being pulled on law enforcement. Typing in Garrison's name, she saw his statistics come up on screen. He was indeed twenty-six years of age, standing a mere six feet two inches tall and a genius. His ability to outwit and outmaneuver his opponents was the reason he had been chose for the sequence. He loved to play games and was a giver of choices.

She pulled up the video file and replayed the footage from the mission. Garrison had been toying with that poor woman who thought she was winning. Garrison was smart and knew what he was doing. Quelly pulled up another one, this time it was Emerson's operation. She watched him hold the young man's shoulder and yank the arm right out of its socket.

Quelly exited the video. That was enough for her. She suddenly felt queasy. These men were not only smart, but strong as well.

Where do you find these guys?

She asked silently to whoever was in charge.

As an agent, she was no stranger to killing. These were a few levels up from her department. In truth, she was an analyst who happened to know a little combat and weaponry.

Bringing the Emerson video file backup, she fast forwarded until it read;

Felps, Raymond B 10:35 p.m.

A grotesque scene was revealed in the car as Felps dug into the man with what appeared to be a pig knife. Finished, he drove the car a few more miles then got out to light the inside on fire with a squeeze bottle of igniter fluid and old fashion matches. He put it in neutral and pushed it over the pass into a deep chasm. The vehicle exploded on impact. Felps made his way down the road but not before leaning against the rail to vomit.

Human after all, huh? Quelly mused.

Kyle lay on the floor still in pain while Landers injected a sedative in his arm. After a little while, his breathing slowed, and the pained look eased away. Childs was trying to wipe the caked blood from his hands as Landers ran his through Kyle's hair.

"Everyone is looking for him. What were you thinking?" Landers turned to him. Childs looked up with deer eyes. "What did you do to him?"

"I," Childs began. "First, we had sex, then…" Landers' hand went up signaling him to not continue. "He was so young, and soft." The look on Landers' face shut him up.

Landers finally stood and stretched. This was not how he wanted to spend the rest of his night. Plus, he had a mission to complete. He turned and saw Childs' mouth open.

"Landers?"

"Hmm?"

"Will he die?" He stared down at Kyle's still body on the floor.

"No." Landers couldn't bear seeing the look of heartache on Childs' face. It made him sick.

"I didn't mean to do this to him. I thought I had killed him, but then he started screaming again." The scene replayed in Childs' mind. "We can't let him die."

Landers grimaced with aggravation. He didn't want to hear about it anymore.

"You know he'll turn you in if given the chance. You may have to kill him anyway."

"No!" Childs yelled. "No, he won't do that. He won't, I'll make sure of it."

"Just leave him be for a while, okay?" Childs was about to touch Kyle then stopped himself. "We have to go in a bit. I have a mission to complete. Be ready."

1:25AM

Landers descended the staircase towards the family room. The son was changing the channel on the television. As the mother came into the room, he shot her three times. A young girl came in and started to scream. A bullet sailed into her forehead. The boy ran into the back of the house. Landers caught him before he could open the door and dragged him back towards the staircase, up to the bedroom. The pain of penetration from Lander's knife into his gut sent a blood curdling scream throughout the house.

Landers washed his hands and combed his hair before going outside. Seeing someone in his car he remembered Childs. In the car, he checked on Kyle who was laying in the back seat still out. There was a medical center for sequence operatives twenty miles from his current location and he decided to take him there.

Kyle lay drugged, sleeping peacefully while Landers talked to the doctor. The secret wing of the government ran hospital was quiet. Only a few patients were admitted, and minimal staff was kept. Landers came back to the reception room and smiled. Childs had cleaned himself up and changed his clothes. His hair, clean and shiny, was brushed to softness. He was wearing a red casual suit with a white muscle tee. The break of dawn seeped through the small windows.

"You look great. Much better."

"How's Kyle? Is he going to be alright?"

Landers nodded. "He should be out in a week. Eugene, don't worry." Childs nodded.

Leaving the hospital, they drove off to their headquarters.

"I'm hungry. Can we stop for a break later?"

Landers laughed. Childs sounded like his name, about to have a temper tantrum.

"Sure we can."

At headquarters, they found the main computer that initiated all the sequences. The printer was going, and all the controls were on. Landers was about to tear off a sheet of information when a gun poked him in the nose. Childs flicked on the lights and the gun lowered. Ilan shielded his eyes.

Eugene, on pins and needles ready to kill, saw who it was and began yelling at him.

"What the hell is wrong with you? If you had actually shot him, we would all be in big shit!"

Ilan stepped back.

"We have to be cautious, remember. Anyway, I came to do a correction on my file."

"Why?" Landers asked.

"I screwed up. Ten minutes turned into thirty seconds because some guy was there and jumped me."

"So, you killed him?" Ilan nodded.

"Don't worry, man," Eugene spoke. "I screwed up too and came here to do the same thing."

"Well, let's get to it before the bureau pages me and finds out our location," Landers interjected. Both men corrected their files under his watch then Landers went to wait in his car while they finished up. As they came out he commanded, "Hurry up! I'm starting to get hungry too."

⌒

Garrison smiled as he walked down the long flight of stairs out of the police precinct. He was now on an unofficial parole and loving the feeling of Munston not being able to harass him. Grinning, he headed for the car and heard Dowan calling his name to wait up. They both got in the car with Emerson as the driver.

"Okay, what now?" He asked.

"Pizza," Garrison replied. The other two agreed.

In the pizza parlor, Emerson restated his question and added, "What are we going to do if we're still in the operation?"

"Do the rest of the sequence."

Garrison sat back pondering over what to say next when Dowan spoke up.

"Our man found Eugene in a forest preserve. Evidently, he had the victim with him still alive, but half dead, in a shed about twenty miles from here. He really screwed up, just like Ilan."

Emerson shook his head in disbelief. "Who told you this, Dowan?"

Dowan pointed a finger behind him and replied, "the man himself."

Garrison and Emerson looked up towards the door and saw Landers, Childs, and Ilan enter the eatery. Garrison raised an eyebrow when Landers came to stand near him.

"Isn't it a little dangerous for you to be seen here with us?"

"Not at all. I'm your quasi parole officer."

Landers winked at them.

"How was your assignment?"

"Fifteen minutes tops," Landers laughed. "Then I had to take Eugene to headquarters only to have Ilan here pull a gun on me."

"How much can one city take?" Munton asked himself out loud.

So many bodies were popping up that the thought of food made his stomach turn. Then he thought about Landers and his mind flamed. Something in his gut told him Landers was linked with the operation running the murders somehow. He wasn't ready to confront him… not yet.

Someone knocked on his office door.

"What is it?"

Landers popped his head in and waved.

"I need the file on Childs, so we can at least find out where he lives."

Munston bent over and flipped through his hard copy files in the desk drawer.

"You don't know?" He jibed while searching.

"No. Why would I?"

When Munston couldn't find the file, he sat up and said, "You deleted the file."

Landers shook his head in bewilderment as Munston used the mouse to wake up his terminal and search the database. On a hunch, Munston had changed the security settings on the data base a few days before to ensure only Landers and himself had authority to make edits.

FILE DOES NOT EXIST flashed across the top of the screen.

Munston looked up at Landers again, his suspicions confirmed. "Is there something you want to tell me?"

"Nothing on him, huh?"

Landers left satisfied that all of Childs data was gone. Even though the men were thorough at headquarters, it never hurt to make sure.

Madison was tired and sluggish because of a cold. The weather was changing, and he wasn't prepared for it. He sat on the roof across the street from his target's house. From there he could see into the kitchen where the girl was eating a bowl of cereal as a late-night snack. In order to get home quick, he took out his sniper rifle and set it on the tripod. He aimed it right between her eyes.

After pulling the trigger, a small 'pink' sounded as the bullet went through the glass and blood splattered on the kitchen wall behind her. Madison got up, packed his gear, and went to his car. It was supposed to take ten minutes. He wasn't in the mood for hanging around that long killing someone. The prisoner she had in the basement was already dead, so he had no reason to retrieve the body. Let the authorities find out what kind of monster she really was.

Landers sat on the couch and opened a can of soda. Madison had a condo that was too large for his belongings. The door opened, and Madison walked in with a bad cough.

"What are you doing here so early?"

Madison just stared at him. "Because I finished early." Another cough made him wince.

"Did you straighten it out?"

"No."

Madison went to the kitchen and boiled some water.

Landers was beginning to think Madison didn't plan to either.

"You're that sick? Why didn't you switch?"

"Martin's in Chicago."

Madison slid down to the kitchen floor and sat there with his head resting on the cabinet door. The next assignment would have to wait.

Ilan checked his mail and found a letter with just his name, no return address. Going into his apartment he opened it and read the message. It was from his employer and sent chills down his entire body.

DUE TO COMPLICATIONS CONCERNING THE OPERATION, YOU ARE NOW TARGETED FOR TERMINATION.

Ilan went into his room, grabbed a few necessities then fled from his apartment. He hopped in his car and drove fast, heading west.

EXPENDABLE ASSETS

Landers was sitting in his office reading a file when a man came in with a letter.

"Special delivery." The man handed it to him and left.

Landers knew from the lettering that it was from his real employer and hurriedly opened it. He read the same message Ilan had and went pale. Munston invaded his line of sight when he bolted for the door and snatched the letter from his hand.

"You don't mind, do you?" Munston read the letter and looked at Landers. "I knew you were in on it."

Landers put on his coat.

"I don't have time for this conversation, Munston. I have to leave if I want to live. I have eighteen hours. Please, let me go. You'll never see me again."

"That's not going to fly, Landers. I'm not letting you just disappear. Not until to you tell me everything."

"I promise you, I will if I live past the next few days."

They locked eyes.

"Please."

Munston saw the desperation in Lander's eyes and moved away from the door. Landers rushed out and down the hallway. Munston followed him with his eyes. When enough time passed for Landers to be out of the building, he went back to his office and wondered where Landers would go. The phone rang and Munston listened as another body was being reported. He was going alone this time. As he was leaving the station, the chief came out of his office to ask about Landers.

"Where'd Landers go at a time like this? I don't take my men going AWOL lightly."

Munston shook his head and didn't answer, leaving the chief in an angered stance.

After inspecting the body at the latest crime scene, Munston sat in his car pondering over whether or not he should report Landers as an accomplice to the murders. He had worked with the man for five years and never knew what he was really like. An officer knocked on the car window, startling him.

"Landers is on the radio."

Munston picked up the communicator.

"Where the hell are you?" He hissed loudly.

"No time. Can't say. They're listening."

"What?" Munston exclaimed. "Who's listening? This is a private police channel!"

There was a short paused.

"They can tap into anything they want. Remember that." Another short pause. "I need you to do me a favor. I know this is asking too much but I need you to check Charles Ilan's apartment. If he's not there, erase his file."

"Why would I do that, Landers?"

"Because he's on the run too."

Landers was at a gas station in Oregon off Interstate 5 drinking a soda when a silver BMW came up and parked next to him. The door opened, and Charles Ilan emerged. Both men looked at each other with a sense of pity. He reached into his car and pulled out another can of soda and offered it to Ilan.

"Where you headed?" Ilan asked as he popped open the can.

"South, then maybe east. You?"

Ilan shrugged.

"Overseas, eventually. But for now," he pulled out a notepad and pen. When he was done writing he turned it around to show Landers.

"Nice state. A little snobbish, but nice."

"How long has it been?"

"Thirty-five hours. But, they're still after us. All of us."

Ilan looked around the cars. "Check yours for any?" Landers nodded.

"All clear."

Eugene was already on the run, with Kyle in tow, when he received his letter. He had gone to his old apartment and found the letter on the floor, making his decision clear. They were headed northbound and he only stopped once to get provisions and make sure Kyle was comfortable. The operation wasn't really after him, per se, since his name and stats had been changed. He no longer had blonde hair either. To be on the safe side, he felt better fleeing.

Kyle woke up as they crossed Idaho's state line. Eugene was eating a cupcake while driving and looking at it made his stomach growl.

He licked his chapped lips and asked, "Can I," Eugene turned to him. "Could I have one…please."

Shocked that Kyle actually said something to him, Eugene nodded.

"Yeah, sure, they're in the bag right next to you." He checked the GPS to see how long before they got to Canada's border.

Ilan had made it to Wyoming and decided to head for Nebraska the next day and stay there for a while. Getting some gas and a supply of junk food, he saw a man in a black sports car staring at him. He played it cool and waved like a good traveler, knowing operation henchmen by sight. Still, he could tell the man wasn't sure about him. His hair was now light brown instead of black and his eyes brown not blue. The man finally drove off because last, but not least, Charles Ilan never wore jeans, t-shirts and leather jackets. Ilan got in his car and smiled. He was safe, for now.

The chief had little patience with Munston's 'I don't know and don't give a damn' attitude regarding Landers and it pissed him off with every minute of every hour of days that went by.

"I wanna know where Landers is, and I wannna' know now!"

"Why would I have that info?"

"Because you were partners for five years! You know something!"

"Look, he left work and never came back. Was he supposed to tip me off on where he was going?"

"Get outta my office!" The chief roared as he stood, finger pointed to the door.

Munston went back to his own office and sat down with a heavy sigh. He was almost on the verge of cracking and telling the chief about Landers. An officer came in, knocking softly on the door frame to get his attention.

"Landers' car was found ditched in Nevada. The vehicle was empty and cleaned out pretty good. Probably won't find anything."

Munston nodded.

Landers was really running for his life.

"Bring it in for dusting just in case."

He started to fear for Landers and wondered where he was now. It had been a little over seventy-two hours and he hoped Landers was alright.

I'm not so innocent in all this either, he chastised himself.

～

Kate parked the car in her driveway and disconnected her phone from the dock. Her brother came up to the car in a huff.

"Mom and dad went out! Want some pizza?" He exclaimed.

"Sure," Kate smiled.

Her little brother was good for something.

While Kate was on the phone with her boyfriend, her brother watched the news. The story was about the countless murders and the struggle to figure out the patterns. He heard a crash outside and jumped up to see what it was. Outside, he found a dark-haired man with a ponytail, wearing a long black trench coat, picking up the pieces that used to be a stone cupid. The man looked up and smiled, then went to his car parked in front of the house. Bobby made a silent 'wow' as the car drove away. It was black as night and very sleek. Going back to finish watching the news he saw the report was over.

A week later, Kate came up the walkway and saw her brother talking to the mystery man. He was gorgeous and didn't seem too much older than her. Turning to leave, the man saw Kate coming up the driveway and smiled. He said goodbye to Bobby and walked right past her. She caught a whiff of clean soap scent then followed him with her eyes. He got into the most beautiful black car. Even when he sped off, she continued to look on; mesmerized.

The man was sitting on the porch next day when Kate got home. She stopped a few feet from him and said, "Hello."

He smiled and returned her greeting with a small wave of his hand.

"I've seen you talking to my brother." Kate started. He nodded and pulled out a cigarette. "Who are you, anyway?"

He lit the cigarette and drew on it. Blowing a ring of smoke, he replied, "A friend."

Kate frowned at that then regained her composure, resuming her sweet smile.

"I meant your name," she laughed.

"Curiosity killed the cat."

"Satisfaction brought him back," she finished the old saying.

"Karl. Are you happy now?"

Kate blushed.

"You're not from around here, are you?"

"*You're* the new addition, not me." He took another drag off his cigarette.

"Those are borderline illegal these days, you know."

She pointed.

"But, not entirely."

Her cheeks flushed red and she immediately snapped out of it when she heard Bobby coming up fast up the walkway.

"Karl!" Bobby yelled as he ran up to them. The man smiled at him and stood. "Hey, where ya' going?"

"Home," Karl laughed. "I just wanted to make sure you got home safely. Are you going to be okay?"

"Yeah. Kate's here now."

Niles walked towards his car and stopped before opening the door in time to see them go into the house. He had scoped the entire place, inside and out.

⌒

Madison was sitting in a chair in a dark, dank room. Beams of sunlight squeezing through the opening of the wooden walls were the only light. A large hand came into view and he felt its impact on his right cheek. There was numbness and his vision blurred for a brief moment. He heard the echo of another hit come from the right of him.

"Well," the male voice drawled. "You two are just screw ups aren'tcha?" Footsteps slapped on the floor and Madison could tell his torturer was pacing. "This one decides the timeline is just a suggestion and doesn't finish the job. Why? Because he was sick and couldn't reach…Martin. And why couldn't he reach him?" There was a long pause. "Because Martin was in Chicago," the man finished in a whining voice. He backhanded them again.

Martin tried to clear his head by shaking it and get a good look at his surroundings. He could barely make out Madison strapped down in the chair next to him.

"The both of yous are getting fried."

Madison and Martin were ushered into a room with leather straps hanging from the beams, two buckets of water and jumper cables. Madison snorted.

So, they're going old school on us.

He started to plan his escape before it was too late.

"Stay cool, dudes," the man sneered and began to laugh loudly.

It was the worst pun Martin ever heard and he too decided he was not going out this way by the hands of that lunatic. He was deep in thought when he felt the jolt of electricity rock his body and convulsed.

If Quelly was a normal concerned citizen she would have turned over evidence of the murders. Instead, she was actually having fun getting the operation goons off

Landers and Ilan's back. She had them being traced in totally different directions. One thing did puzzle her and that was why Niles had not made his move yet. So he snooped around, got friendly with Bobby and flirted with that skank sister. Of course, he would be targeted soon after. Quelly had him covered though.

Suddenly, she remembered Martin and Madison's bad situation. Her fingers went flying across the virtual keypad and finding the main power of the building they were being held in, shut it down.

The power died, and everyone got confused, except Martin and Madison. They took the opportunity to slip out of the straps and fight their way out of the makeshift torture chamber. As they reached safety in a nearby field, both men stopped to catch their breath.

"That was really freaky." Martin gasped.

"An answer to our prayers, if you ask me."

"How the fuck did we get here?"

"Come on. Let's get out of here before they catch on and come after us. They're not that stupid if they're in the operation."

Quelly cut the power back on then and smiled at herself. One advantage about everything being linked by a super computer was the stuff you could get away with at the push of a button.

Munston looked through all of Landers' car along with the other specialists. The officer was right. It was cleaned thoroughly. The entire vehicle had been washed, waxed and vacuumed, trunk included. He suddenly felt like this case was more serious than he could handle. He walked over to another detective who seemed to be scrutinizing it more than the others.

"Any idea where he might be headed?"

The detective turned to look up at him, green eyes gleaming.

"No. But maybe you do."

Munston instantly felt a sense of fear and backed away from the man. Something wasn't right about him and when he caught a glimpse of the I.D. badge he realized the name didn't match the person.

"Alright guys! Let's pack it up!" He commanded.

He got in his car and waited to make sure everyone had finished up then drove off. In his rear-view mirror, he saw the green-eyed detective get in his car and follow him at a safe distance.

"Shit!" Munston slammed his hand on the dash.

∽

Kate was in the house by herself with Karl and she felt a little awkward. It was her idea to let him in the house to watch television, even though she had making out in mind. She could later brag to her friends about snagging a much older guy. His hand, which had been rubbing her thigh, began to feel rough and painful. The rubbing got so hard that she wanted to cry out.

He suddenly cut off the television and the room went dark. She could feel his hand under her mini skirt then her panties being ripped off in one yank. He pushed her down on the couch and shoved the panties in her mouth, gagging her as she kicked and struggled. The only thing she could see clearly were his eyes as he forced his manhood into her roughly, tearing into her as if he were trying to kill her. Her screams muffled, she tensed up her body to try and make it hurt him more than her.

She felt him ejaculate and pull out of her. He sat atop her for a moment, those eyes glaring down, then began to punch her in the face, in the ribs, the stomach, every place he could catch a spot as she tried to get away by squirming around. With every blow she made sure to give one back, so he knew she was not going down lightly.

Kate woke up in pain and forced her one glassy eye to focus on her surroundings, the other eye swollen shut. She was in the spare bedroom slumped against the far wall. He had chased her through the house and caught her several times, raping and beating her repeatedly until the early hours of the morning. Slowly, she got up, hunched over, and headed for the front door. As she entered the hallway, she heard her name being called. Turning to the direction of the voice, she saw Karl at the other end. He ran towards and in the nick of time, her leg muscles unlocked. She took off through the kitchen and out the front door.

Outside, in the middle of the street, she realized she was screaming and clamped a hand over her mouth. She slowed down her run as tears streamed down her bruised face. Her friend lived across the street, so she banged furiously on the door, waiting for someone to answer. Out of the corner of her eye, she saw Karl walk calmly out of her house and get into his car. He rolled down the window and blew her a kiss as her friend's door swung open.

Kate sat on the examination table waiting for her friend, Cari, to come back. She was a mess from head to toe with cuts, bruises and welts all over her body. Cari had a cup of water in her hand when she returned with a nurse.

"Your mother is here. You can go home now, if you like," the nurse said.

Kate just sat still sipping on the water to cool her throbbing lips. Her mother came in and began to cry when she saw her. She knew her mother was angry. Kate was no angel. Her mother loved her regardless. Her mother cleared her throat.

"Honey, come on. Let's go. You're going to stay with Cari until we get the house cleaned up." She helped Kate slowly slide off the hospital bed.

The pain was almost unbearable, but she refused to let it show, not even to her mother. She made her way down the hall and felt her mother and Cari had stopped a few feet behind her.

"I really want to thank you for being there," her mother said to Cari. "You'll take care of her?" Cari nodded. "Thank you." She said again and went to sign Kate out.

Munston had a feeling that the rapist was tied to the murders somehow. He just needed some kind of proof and hoped his crew could find it. Every victim so far had been linked to some shady, underground operation that dealt with Bi-Genetics. He did come across some footage from a party that took place a few months before and the victim was in it. Her younger brother being the center of attention. What he saw, made him feel ill.

Cunt got what she deserved. He thought to himself. *What is wrong with these people?*

His door opened, and the lunch cart came rolling in with his order. Taking a bite of his sandwich he leaned back and closed his eyes.

Greg Madison and Quinn Martin were having late dinner at a Chinese restaurant. The five-hour drive to the next state was worth it. Quinn stopped eating for a moment.

"What do you want to do now? It's still early in the game and we have plenty of money."

Greg looked at him and shrugged.

"Does it really matter? Personally, I want to sleep off this cold."

"Great way to start off a new year, huh?"

"Oh yeah. On the run and loving it."

"On that note," Quinn motioned at the door.

Two men entered the restaurant, noticeable bulges under their suit jackets. Quinn knew at once they were looking for Greg and himself. Grabbing Greg by the arm, he headed out the back way through the kitchen. He made sure to leave enough money for the meal and a big fat tip.

Childs got out of the car and looked at the flat he had rented in advance for the next few months. He helped Kyle out of the car and they both went inside. Kyle seemed surprised by his taste in décor. Everything was clean lines and modernistic. Eugene pulled out his new mobile device and ordered dinner from a nearby restaurant for delivery. After that, he picked up his gun, released the safety and aimed it at Kyle while the other hand held out the phone. Kyle stopped eating the bag of corn chips and stared at Eugene in terror.

"Call your mother." Kyle went stiff and Eugene knew what he was thinking. "It's alright. No one can trace the call."

Kyle grabbed the mobile phone from Eugene's hand with visibly shaking ones and cautiously dialed his home number. It rang four times before someone answered it and he heard his mother's voice. Clearing his throat, he spoke.

"Hi, Mom. It's me."

There was an eerie silence.

"My god, Kyle. Where are you, honey?" Her tone was falsely kind, sending shivers down his spine.

"I can't tell you but I'm alright. Don't worry about me."

Eugene took the phone from him and disconnected the call while putting the gun down. He knew how hard that was for Kyle to speak so calmly to that woman and was proud of him. The whole idea was to send the mother a message by taking away her only son. It wasn't until later that Childs found out she didn't give a rat's ass about Kyle because he was a Bi-Genetic. She kept up the grieving mother appearance for the media. He felt sick watching it and couldn't imagine what Kyle felt when he saw that press conference.

A stack of boxes sat waiting for him to unpack and he set off to do it. The doorbell chimed thirty minutes later, and he came back into the kitchen with dinner.

The two cleared off the table so they could set and arrange the food, let alone eat. As Eugene sat down he noticed the open can of soda sitting by Kyle. He reached over and picked it up.

"Did you drink any of this?"

"No," Kyle started. "Well, a sip." He saw Eugene's lips purse. "I lost my nerve though!"

Eugene handed him the container of fried rice and dug around in the bags for some bottled water.

"Just in case you took more than a sip. The doctor told you no carbonated drinks for the next three weeks." He found a bottle of water and set it down in front of Kyle. "You're drinking this for the rest of the day."

While they were eating, Eugene's phone rang, causing Kyle to jump with fright. Eugene knew who it must be and was correct in his assumption. Wiping his mouth, he answered the phone.

"I'm eating, make it quick."

The other end of the line was silent for what seem like minutes then an irritated voice.

"I was the one able to clean up your mess. You should

be more appreciative." Winters spoke in his usual dead-pan tone.

"Sorry. What's up?"

He got up and moved to a different room.

"The district is checking on all new residents, so they are coming to check on Robert Stevens later. Remember, you've never been to the city before. And hide Kyle."

Winters hung up and Eugene got the point. He went to have a chat with Kyle.

Landers sat down on the motel room's bed exhausted and hungry from the long ride. Digging into one of the shopping bags he found a can of soda, a sandwich and a bag of chips. That would be his dinner and he wolfed it down in record time. He didn't dare leave the room even though he was still hungry afterwards. On the television was a report on the murders followed by an interview with the investigator handling the case. Munston was coming out of the precinct pushing and yelling. Landers laughed a little at that, then shut the screen off. Someone was knocking on the door.

Landers grabbed his gun and eased towards the window. He flipped a small corner up and saw two men in black suits standing outside his door. Ready to take them out he removed the safety and slowly stood. Then he noticed Winters and cursed.

"I was ready to kill all of you!" He hissed flinging the door open. "Why don't you guys wear a different color?"

Winters and his two subordinates walked into the motel room and he looked around the perimeter with distaste. He even swiped the dresser with one index finger and used a Kleenex to wipe it off.

"Have you contacted anyone in the past few days?" His greyish blue eyes had sparks flying around in them, a trick of the light.

"Umm, no. I'm on the run, remember? Why would I?" Landers watched him sit down in the only chair in the room and stare at him.

"Then how does your partner know you are involved?"

"Because he's not stupid, that's why!" Landers spat.

The doorbell rang while Eugene was cleaning up and he stopped his chores to answer it. Taking a deep breath, he opened the door and laid eyes on a tall slender man in a dark grey suit.

"Yes? May I help you?" Eugene asked staring the man right in the face.

"I'm just coming through the neighbor to welcome any new comers in the area. City protocol, you see."

"Oh? Well that's mighty kind of you." Eugene said in a pleasant southern drawl.

"It says here you have a wife."

"Oh, yes. She's not feeling too good. It was a long trip and the city is a bit exhausting."

"Of course. Well, have a good night and welcome to Manhattan."

"Thank you much. Good night."

Eugene closed the door and slumped against it as he took the wire rimmed glasses off and let out another deep breath. He went to the bedroom to check on Kyle who was asleep in female form in case the man asked to see her.

She was directly in the middle of the bed wearing nothing except one of Eugene's t-shirts which was big enough to cover past her hips. He sat down on the edge of the bed and watched her for a while. After what seemed like seconds, he looked up at the clock and realized he had been sitting there for fifteen minutes. Kyle had rolled over in her sleep without him even noticing.

Eugene got up and went to the bathroom, so he could get ready for bed himself. His phone light up as he crept gently into bed and under the covers. He answered quickly. A voice that sounded much like Landers could be heard in the background before Winters came on.

"How did it go?"

"It went fine," Eugene sighed loudly. "He rattled off some bullshit about a welcoming committee and city protocol. Is that Landers with you?"

There was that infamous dramatic long silence then, "It could be. I will contact you again soon." Eugene could hear a fight going on before Winters hung up.

In their line of business, trust was not given freely. Childs didn't trust Winters. Never did.

Niles was sitting in his new car eating a container of ice cream when the grey car pulled up next to his. The windows rolled down and the passenger wearing a black suit and sunglasses leaned out.

"Where have you been, Niles? Hiding from us?"

The man took off his sunglasses and grinned.

"If I were hiding from you, would I still be here calmly talking to you?"

"You didn't report in."

"There was a police officer snooping around, and I did report it to Winters."

The man picked up his mobile and dialed on it. Niles stopped paying attention and resumed eating his ice cream. It was melting.

"Okay Niles, you're clear."

The car pulled off at the same moment his mobile rang. The code was unique to Winters.

Niles set his ice cream on the passenger seat and answered, "What is it?"

Winters apparently didn't like his tone of voice.

"Hello?" Niles spoke into the mic.

He was about to hang up when Winters finally spoke.

"I don't know who you think I am, but don't ever use that tone of voice with me. It pisses me off and I will have you terminated in your sleep." Niles rolled his eyes. "Where are you?"

"In my car," Niles replied sweetly.

"Don't fuck with me, Niles. Tread lightly."

"In front of my house, where else." Niles lied. *Fuck him.*

"Get to headquarters for a meeting."

Winters hung up as did Niles.

The meeting was already in progress when Winters arrived, and everyone turned to look at him accusingly. He sat down near the entrance.

"Proceed. Don't mind me."

"We can't keep them misled forever," an agent continued. "Giving the boss false information and monkeying with the government servers is getting old."

"Yes, we can. Until they get off the others' tails." Another agent replied.

"A little warning to all of you. Don't jabber at the mouth or you won't have one anymore."

A mobile rang and one of the head officers reached into his inside breast pocket and answered it.

"Jeremiah?" His face scrunched up in puzzlement.

Winters got up and snatched the mobile from the officer's hand. He knew who it was before the man could speak; their employer.

CAUGHT UP

The police chief unconsciously gnawed on his thumb nail, having regressed to a childhood nervous condition. He sat at the end of the dark wood table in planning director's home library that had been set up as a meeting room. Around it, the rest of the sector leaders were scattered, some standing others sitting slumped in their seats. There was a morbid sense of defeat permeating the room.

Death had taken hold of the Grid City and it was blatant to them the reason why, when looking at the victims. None of them were immune and that was a problem needing a resolution. The house servant came in with a tray of glasses accompanied by a large bottle of whiskey.

"Thank you, dear," the director said. "You may leave for the day."

The servant gave a small bow and left the room.

When everyone had a glass filled to their desired pour, they all took a seat; And a swig.

"How are we going to combat this one, people?" The city attorney started.

"My God! Murder? Isn't that a bit extreme for the issue?" The Mayor exclaimed.

The chief slammed his glass on the table and stared them one by one, slack jawed.

"Are you serious? After what we agreed upon? We

essentially authorized crimes against children and guaranteed no action would be taken against those who engaged."

The others blanched at his outburst. They didn't dare give a rebuttal, knowing he spoke the truth.

"Well, it's too late now," the director snapped. "How do we resolve this?"

"Shut it all down," the Section five leader replied softly.

"That's impossible!" the city attorney leaned forward with his eyes narrowed. "Do you know how many dens are established?"

"Doesn't matter. We need to start immediately. Go by sectors if necessary."

"The sooner, the better," the chief muttered.

"I say we request authorization to leave the city for a few months," the director said.

"You mean run away from the mess you helped create?" Sector five's leader asked vehemently.

"There are killers going after anyone involved in the underground markets! We aren't the ones doing those sick things!" the city attorney moved from his angry lean forward to abruptly standing. His fists were clenched tight.

"We may not do the harm, but we were the catalyst," the Mayor said.

She slumped back in her chair and watched the others go silent. The attorney slowly settled back in his seat with a blank stare on his face. Another round of drinks was poured, and they sipped in silence.

～

Older model sedans pulled up in front of the safe house and Winters felt his eyes narrow with disgust. The only reason anyone would use those relics was to avoid being traced, the vehicles having outdated computer systems. He recognized the men exiting them as government henchmen under direct orders of the Defense Secretary. They were there to help facilitate the shutting down of rogue agents along with disreputable establishments. He concluded the sector leaders thought themselves helping the situation, not knowing it would get much worse.

A behemoth of a man came towards him. At least six feet five with all muscle, the man carried himself like an authoritarian. Brown suspenders peeked from under his suit jacket along with an old school 9mm Glock. His duty issue was strapped in a holster on the other side. Light brown hair cut short was slicked back neatly for an unobstructed view of dark blue eyes that reminded Winters of a storm.

Modern cowboy. Shit!

"Winters, I take it?"

The man stepped up to him and they clasped each other's hand in a vice grip. They held on for a moment, sizing the other up.

"Agent Holmes."

Winters cocked his head and lifted an eyebrow.

"Like the famous detective?"

His voice dripped with sarcasm.

"Oh, I'm better than that." Holmes mouth spread into a Cheshire grin.

When they release their handshake, the rest of Holmes men came to stand behind him. All wore dark suits and ties and their hair looked like they had just rolled out of bed in a scramble.

"Last minute deployment?"

Winters nodded towards them.

"This place gave us no choice."

"We are handling it."

"Really? Cuz, there's a lot of dead bodies and a whole bunch of unsavory shit going on."

"I would appreciate if you and your men followed my lead."

Winters couldn't stop his eyes from blinking rapidly as he struggled not to show frustration.

"Of course." Holmes step closer. "Until I deem it necessary to intervene."

The entourage walked passed Winters into the safe house and he stayed in place, not looking behind him to see when the last one was inside. He took out his ear bud commlink and placing it in his ear, pressed. A small click sounded.

"We may have a problem."

His grey eyes turned a dark steely hue as he looked out at the horizon.

A small faction within Holmes group gave Winters that not so fuzzy feeling as he listened to them talk shit about government assassins being glorified pussies, their demeanor turning hostile as he walked by. He went to meet back up with Holmes.

"Who are they?" He gestured towards the men.

Holmes turned around and made a disgusted face when he saw them.

"Third party contractors. Government pays them, but they are not one of us."

"That's obvious." Winters stared up at the safe house, lost in thought. "Is there going to be a problem?"

"Not if I can help it."

"Then you're going to need a tighter leash."

Winters went ahead of Holmes into the house and directly up the stairs to the second floor. He turned in the bedroom farthest down the hall and plopped down on the bed. His head felt like it was being pounded, making his eyes hurt. Thinking about the current situation reaffirmed his assessment that it was not kosher. The Defense Secretary had dispatched a team to handle some of their own assassins and didn't even know it. There were Shadowmen embedded all over the world in key positions.

This was going to get messy.

He laid there listening to the muffled buzz of his phone vibrated in his jacket pocket until he knew whoever was on the other end would get annoyed. Removing it, he hit the accept icon.

"What's the status?" The man's voice asked.

"This needs to be over and done soon. Too many variables."

"And too many nosy fuckers getting in our way."

He snorted at that. Couldn't agree more.

"By the way," the man continued. "Have you been compromised?"

Winters' eyes went wide in anger. He abruptly sat up as his face contorted in anger.

"Do you think I would still be here if that were the case?"

"No need to be so …"

"Don't you ever ask me that again!"

"Winters."

He disconnected the call before the man could finish. The possibility was high that was the case. Unless either side played their hand, he refused to expose himself.

Holmes knocked on the door frame, and devious grin on his face.

"I have a list of persons needing private counseling."

"You mean a kill list."

"Not necessarily. Depending on what they say, we can negotiate long vacations. Out of my country."

His expression grew dark.

"Is that right?"

"I don't want any more bloodshed than you do."

Wrong. I want an ocean of blood running through the streets. Winters thought in reply.

For three weeks the two men hunted down the assassins on the list, finding only two. Both were collected, tortured and bagged for international travel. Winters played his part, letting Holmes and his men do their thing while giving signals to the captured so they wouldn't be killed. Neither gave the one piece of information Holmes needed; their employer. Winters didn't feel the least bit obligated to tell him that none of them knew. He did.

A few more agents were found, and Winters was given the names. As he scanned the list on his phone, Holmes came up next to him and pointed at one of them.

"This one we are going to approach a little different. Give him an incentive to talk more.

Winters felt his blood cool with a sense of fear and foreboding.

He did not like this way of doing things. To confirm his suspicions, the next one they killed. And it wasn't Holmes men who did so. The third-party agents he categorized as animals, enjoying the murder of their fellow man with extreme prejudice. Not good. He began to figure out a new exit strategy before it was too late.

Enroute to the next one, he sat silently in the armored luxury vehicle next to Holmes who perused his tablet with intense concentration. They pulled up to a modest home, painted white with a small yard of well-kept grass. There was movement inside and Winters felt his stomach drop.

He eyed the third-party men as everyone exited the vehicles. He counted at least ten agents, including himself and knew it was too many. Holmes seemed to feel the same way as he too glanced at the four contract killers.

"Let's try to keep this toned down, shall we?"

He addressed it to them more so than Winters.

"As long as everyone behaves," one of them said, laughingly.

Sunlight bore down on the black car, desperate to penetrate the dark tint. Niles leaned back in the driver's seat thanking the Gods for them. He was a night person by nature and having to be up so early pained him. It was nearly noon; the pinnacle of daytime and the bane of his existence. Blue light blinking from his right made him look over at the passenger seat. His phone shimmied around, and he stared at it for a bit, seeing the number. Sitting upright, he adjusted the small tub of ice cream in his left hand and reached for it. He accepted the call and it filtered through the car speakers.

"What now?"

There was a long pause on the other end.

"You really don't want to piss me off today, Niles," Winters' voice said.

He could hear the passive aggressiveness in the man's tone. Niles rolled his eyes.

"Where are you?"

"In my car." Niles smirked as another pause came.

"Don't…"

"I'm eating ice cream. You want me to bring you some?"

"I need you to get to my location right now," Winters demanded.

"What for?" Niles frowned. "Am I going on the run too?"

"Just get here. Now!"

The call disconnected, and Niles let out a loud sigh. He didn't want to go running for the sake of covering his employer's ass. His ice cream was melting so he finished it off and hit the ignition. Coordinates downloaded onto his navigation system.

"Guess I should go. Don't want to get his panties in a bunch."

When he pulled into the driveway of the safe house, he grimaced at its the shoddy condition. Then he spotted multiple vehicles hidden along the back side. He controlled his breathing and walked casually to the front door. Laughter from a small child erupted followed by giggling. Alarms went off in his head. He wrapped his hand around the knob and flung the door wide open.

The foyer was occupied by ten men, some sitting, the others standing around an antique sofa. In the center was Winters playing catch with a little girl. The rubber ball barely fit in her hands. He counted more guns than people in the room. Winters gave him a signal with his eyes to remain calm.

"Daddy!"

His daughter looked over at him smiling wide. As she moved to go to him, the man next to Winters clasped his hands around her shoulders, stopping her.

"Remember, we need to talk to your dad first. Then you can come back and play all you want."

"Okay!" He let her continue playing with ball.

"Let my daughter go," Niles demanding through gritted teeth.

"She's here to make sure you cooperate," Holmes said.

"No. She goes, or nothing happens."

"Niles," Winter interrupted. "We want this to go smoothly."

"Fuck that," one of the contract killers blurted out.

"Let's just get on with it."

"You don't get a say in this!" Holmes seethed.

"What the hell are we doing here then?"

His daughter's face scrunched up at the men's quick succession arguments. Winters pulled her away and held her firm in front of him.

"He'll talk if she's gone, right?" Another contractor spat.

A split second. Niles calculated that's how long it took the man to raise his gun, lean over Holmes and put the gun to her head. Niles and Holmes expression turned to horror, Winters turning to the man.

"No!" Winters yelled as Niles' daughter looked up at her father.

"Daddy?"

He heard the gun fire. Everything went black.

Screaming. Lots of screaming. And rapid fire.

Everything felt wet and sticky. His throat burned as if he had eaten fire. There was movement all around him. Whenever something came close, he lashed out, grabbing hold and tearing through it. Something hit him hard. When he didn't go down, arms took hold squeezing and didn't let go. His vision returned.

He was screaming and not the only one. Blood splatter was everywhere, on the side of the house, in the flower-beds, the grass. Bodies were strewn along the yard. Some halfway out the front door.

"Niles! I need you to get out of here. Now!"

He was released and fell to the grass. Garrison stood over him flecks of blood on his face. A gun in each hand. Out of the corner of his eye he spotted a unit with assault rifles advance from vehicles at the end of the driveway. Garrison pulled him to his feet and tossed him to the side as a hail of bullets came flying, hitting him squarely.

"No!" Niles screamed as he tried to get to Garrison.

"No!" He saw Garrison give him a smile before his eyes closed. "Ahhh! Motherfucker!"

"You have to go!" Winters' voice grated in his ears.

With utter abandon and nothing left to lose, Niles turned on the now spread out unit and took out the two nearest him barehanded. Whenever the one tried to get up from his assault, he used the butt of the man's own rifle to knock him back down while keeping an iron grip on the other. The soldier now knocked out, he commenced to pulling on his captive's arm, ignoring the screams as it tore from the socket. His vision went blank, like white noise.

Winters shot two of the government soldiers coming at him in the head and before they hit the ground, went to retrieve Niles. He had to pass Garrison's body splayed across a flowerbed and gritted his teeth in frustration. This was not supposed to happen. He charged through the cross hairs of bullets flying and shot the man in Niles grip, putting him out of his misery. Then he hit Niles harder than he had ever hit anyone in his life. At first, Niles was stunned, his grip slipping. He went down like an elephant, his eyes glazed over. A car screeched to a halt next to them and Winters hauled Niles off the ground and into it. Two men jumped out and grabbed Garrison's body.

"Go!"

It went careening off into the distance and Winters stood alone, breathing heavily, covered in blood. The click of a gun behind him made him correct his posture. He turned, weapon raised and stared into a wounded Holmes' eyes. The two men didn't waver.

"Cease fire!" The backup unit's commander called out.

Holmes squinted to alleviate the blood in his right eye. His leg was bent as if he had dragged it along, a large patch of blood soaked through the shoulder of his white button-down shirt.

"I need you to stand down, Winters."

"Or what?"

He could see the man contemplating what to do. Either way, he would do no such thing. And he would take everyone in the vicinity out as he left because he wasn't dying today. Holmes must have understood his expression and demeanor. They lowered their weapons at the same time and Holmes tapped the side of his head with the butt of his gun.

"I am so sorry. This isn't…"

"It's too late for that."

An agent came stumbling out of the house.

"What do we do with the little girl's body?"

Winters looked over and saw the edge of her frilly flowered dress moving softly in the breeze. Without thinking, he shot the agent in the eye. His body flew backwards and landed flat on the floor inside the house.

"Goddamn it!" Holmes cried as he attempted to raise his gun at Winters.

Weapons were trained on him and Winters smirked, dropping his gun in the grass. Inside the house, one of his own agents lifted the little girl off the floor and carried her out.

They can't have her. I won't let them. Niles.

For the first time in years, Winters felt pain. This loss was too much.

President Lynmore grabbed hold of George by the front of his shirt and pulled him close. Her face was contorted with rage as the two stood in the middle of the Oval office.

"You let those third-party goons murder a child? A fucking infant, for Christ's sake!"

He didn't need to say anything. The look of agony and shame said plenty and all she needed to know. She let go, pushing him away from her.

"How is this being handled?"

George straightened his suit and cleared his throat.

"We circulated news that the family moved due to the rise in murders. The entire place is packed up, sitting empty."

"Anything in there to clue us in on the assassin, Niles?"

"Nothing. Just an ordinary home of a single father raising a five-year-old little girl."

"The nanny?" When he didn't answer, she felt hot again. "And what explanation do we have for that?"

"Car accident while running errands. We planted the body at the scene once it was done being set up."

The President inhaled deep and let it out slow. She paced the office, her fingers running along her necklace chain. Her secret service agents stood nervously in the four points of defense. George dropped his large frame onto the loveseat and leaned back until he almost lay flat, one hand covering his face.

"What does Holmes say?"

Without moving his hand, he replied.

"There was a second group helping the assassins. They had to be waiting somewhere close after what happened with the previous men his team interrogated."

"Interrogated? Hmph!" The President turned to him. "Let's not sugar coat what we were doing. Can we find this Niles person?"

"Oh, I doubt that," he said, sitting up to let his hand fall to his sides. "And I don't want to after what he did to those men."

"Well, we can't blame him for that. If it were me, I'd have killed every last one of you." She sat at her desk, arms stretch across it. "Now what?"

"We wait and see. The list is a bust. No more information is forthcoming on their locations."

"So, we just wait for more murders to happen?"

"They have stopped. Which is a whole new wrinkle."

"How so?" The President asked.

"Why did they stop? Have they met their agenda? Too many unanswered questions." George replied.

"Then find them and get this done!"

George got up and left the room, followed by two secret service agents. He felt anxious and angry. Watching the mission feeds made his heart hurt. He should have listened to his gut when the team commander brought up contract killers. The image of Niles daughter would never leave his mind, and rightly so.

I fucked this up!

An armored vehicle waited for him outside and he hurried into it, careful not to let any of the press catch a photo op. With stealth and ease, his bodyguards were right behind him. They settled in the back seat and he pressed the communication button on the armrest.

"Take me to the holding facility."

"You got it," the driver replied.

He was due to have a chat with that Winters character.

Reports regarding the safe house incident came flooding into the main facility's database, leaving the leaders baffled at the outcome. The telepath swung back and forth in his chair as he watched all the feeds on the giant vidscreen across from his desk. Between the Shadowmen Organization, the U.S government and the aliens, there was no contest as to who was worst. They were all a royal mess.

He understood why Winters had the girl's body taken. She would have been a science specimen. Niles documents contained fascinating tidbits into his true nature. The way he tore those men apart in a fit of rage, his mind probably a blank slate the whole time, was enough alone to be studied. The incident put a constraint on their timeline.

Time to intervene.

Above the feed sat the communications icon. He tapped the glass surface of his desk and a virtual keyboard appeared. Moving the arrow towards it, he clicked to open a video chat screen. In his list of contacts, he found Dr. Vasence's, now Professor, direct line at Facility three. It connected instantly, as if he had been waiting for the call.

"You monster, I knew it," Professor Vasence said. His face appeared in the empty frame.

"Then this won't take long. I need clearance for your dungeon."

Vasence took a bite from the fruit he was eating and chewed slowly. Behind him, two of his assistants were holding down an already restrained patient, the third going deep in the abdomen with a scalpel.

"You know, they have anesthesia for those kinds of procedures," the telepath suggested.

"Mmm," the Professor swallowed. "Then we couldn't gauge his pain threshold."

"And I'm a monster?"

"This is purely for scientific research. What's your excuse?"

"How is next week?"

The telepath brought the conversation back on track.

"Fine. Make sure you don't use the main entrance. I will get coordinates to you for a direct portal into my lab."

"Bartley will not be happy."

"Who's going to tell him?"

"I'll be in touch."

He disconnected the call right as the surgeon pulled out a section of intestine. Every faction believed they were not the enemy, yet they did barbaric things like that, negating the argument. All for research. All for the greater good. For the advancement of humanity.

Bullshit.

As promised, he received the portal info when he arrived at the facility. He was taken aback by the sight of Facility three now above water, a floating city of advanced technology exposed to the prying eyes of the world. From the far end of the lowest building he went through and found himself in Professor Vasence's dark labs. Black walls and floors with electric blue accents made him feel like he had entered a video game. The only difference was that beyond those dark tinted walls were Bi-Genetics with powerful talents and those who were more suited for combat than college.

Professor Vasence came up behind him and stood in the main corridor. His eyes had an odd gleam to them, making the telepath assume the man had taken some-thing he shouldn't. Then he spotted the tiny flecks of blood on his labcoat and realized the look was elation.

Professor Vasence was drunk off an experiment that entailed a live subject.

"Nice of you to come greet me personally, it wasn't necessary, though."

"Nonsense! I wanted to see which ones you pick."

"Does it matter?"

"Of course it does. I have to decide if certain measures need to be implemented or not."

"I am not taking any of your dangerous pets. Only the well-trained ones."

"No faith in the S.O. or the government?"

"You?"

Professor Vasence began walking down the hall. His steps not making a sound.

"I never did," he replied.

The facilities Chairman stood facing the observation window of the conference room while he watched the wildlife surrounding the region. Soft wind rustled the foliage as the afternoon sun started to dip. Life was uncomplicated on the island. A notification beep echoed across the room and he turned to the vidscreen on the wall.

"Agent Talbot is requesting permission to enter the conference room," the female receptionist said.

"He has clearance. Why have you stopped him?"

"Because, you said," she paused and looked down. "You said not to disturb you until dinner."

"Oh. My apologies. Send him here."

Thirty minutes later, the telepath walked in wearing a grim expression. He understood completely. The incident feed was gruesome and avoidable. As a human it sickened him.

"I take it, you have activated a new phase in the plan."

"That is correct. We need to get this done so we can go on to the next."

The Chairman stepped down from the platform and went to sit at the table. Talbot sat across from him. Silence engulfed them, both thinking deeply about the situation at hand.

"It was never going to go smoothly," the chairman finally said.

"And there's no one to blame." The telepath saw the man's incredulous look. "As far as the execution. Humans are the culprit."

"Are you going to tell me?"

"It may be better if I don't. Once the government moves on the grid, we will have a small window. Plus, we have no idea what those aliens are up to."

The Chairman remembered seeing a feed of the female amazon. Her eyes were that of a predator who found a giant nest of edible fare. Earth was in dire need of a savior since its people couldn't do the job. Those four aliens were not the answer.

"The moment the sequence is complete, we will start. Society gets no warning or reprieve."

Talbot nodded in agreement.

CHAPTER FOUR

WOLVES IN THE CABINET

Palmer Holding Facility was a secret maximum-security prison used by the government for information extraction; by any means. It was completely off the books and not the only one in the world. A joint venture with each nation was approved to have them built considering the planet's troubles.

The Homeland Secretary watched it get closer as the vehicle rolled towards the main gate. From a normal perspective, it looked like anyone could just walk in. Barbed wire fences went out decades ago in exchange for laser sensors. If an unauthorized guest crossed the checkpoint, they would be fried crispy. About one hundred tiny dots lined the height of the gates on each side where the lasers created a lined grid.

His window was rolled down for him to show his I.D to the guard.

"Good evening, Homeland Secretary. Welcome back to Palmer."

"Thank you, soldier. Carry on."

The soldiers saluted him as his vehicle went forward through the gates. Palmer was massive, and it would take another five minutes to drive to the desired wing's entrance. Anxiousness filled him. He was about to have a conversation with someone that, in his book, was a dangerous genius. For all they knew, he could be the mastermind. On his tablet was the report on Holmes' findings after daily interactions with him. The picture of Winters disturbed him. Like he should know him. He hoped to God not.

At the south wing entrance, another set of guards awaited him to do the same protocol. This time, he got out of the vehicle and tapped his keycard on the door panel. Giant mechanisms whirred, and the fifty-foot metal doors eased open. Inside was an industrial lift. His two bodyguards and himself boarded and were sealed in. It shot down eight floors then made a gentle stop. When it opened, a soldier stood before them. He gave a salute and pivoted until his back was to them.

They quietly followed him down the corridor lined with windowless metal doors. At the turn, the cells became clear glass enclosures for the guards to see every corner. These were only on one side to eliminate communication with other prisoners. At the tenth one in, the group stopped in front of Winters's holding cell. The soldier held his keycard up to the scanner and the cell unlocked.

"Let me know when you're done, sir." Then, he left.

"Wait here," he commanded his bodyguards.

Winters sat cross legged on the single bed set against the far wall. His jet-black hair was disheveled, resembling a jungle lion's mane. He seemed comfortable in light blue scrubs and bare feet. There was no movement from the man as the Defense Secretary dragged the chair in and set it before him. He adjusted his suit as he sat and stared at Winters.

"Are we going to have a nice chat or is this a silent combat?"

A smile formed on Winters face. His eyes conveyed something sinister. He unhooked his hands in his lap and let them fall flat beside him.

"You think I'm the mastermind."

"And I'm wrong." That smile widened. "What is the agenda? Murdering people is never a good plan."

Darkness formed in Winters expression. His head fell back against the wall.

"Is that not your plan? Tit for tat. Murder the killers without asking why?"

"Your people are nothing but vigilantes. How are we different?"

"Tell me," Winters raised his head. "Do you think any of those victims were capable of changing their ways?"

George squirmed in his seat. They both knew the answer. He had no love loss for the corrupt underbelly of the grid city. Instead of remorse, they would be resentful and cause more damage. Even so, it still didn't make it right.

"We are not saints or saviors," Winters said.

He seemed to have read George's mind.

He didn't notice Winters leap off the bed towards him. The restraints went taunt, stopping him mere inches from his startled face. Up close, staring into those grey eyes, George felt his blood run cold. This man was no ordinary killer. Outside the cell, his bodyguards reached for their weapons. He held up a hand, signaling them to stand down.

"Mankind is a disease. But I will not let it be wiped out by our own foolishness."

Winters stood straight and backed away, sitting back on the bed in his original position.

"We have ways to get information out of our prisoners."

George heard the wobble in his voice and cursed himself inwardly.

"Oh? Have you ever tortured a Shadow agent? It's counterproductive at best."

"Is that what you are?"

"Who's to say." He cocked his head to the side.

"Maybe."

In that moment, George knew he was something much more. Interrogation would not work on him. He needed a different approach. As if understanding his thinking, Winters gave him a nod.

"I look forward to whatever you figure out."

"Don't worry, I'll make it worth your while."

He got up and took the chair out with him. The soldier from before was already coming. His bodyguards must have hit the call button. Another look at Winters, he saw the man's eyes were closed as he went into a meditation.

For two days, George was in a funk, trying to get his head around the enigma that was Winters. While he sat in the Oval office, his attention wavered from what the President was saying.

"Why are you not listening to me?" She yelled.

He snapped out of it and found her standing over him like a vulture.

"My apologies, Madam President."

"So?"

"I beg your pardon?"

"What was he like? You did go see him, correct?"

"Truthfully?" She pursed her lips at that. "He's worse than any monster I have ever encountered."

"How did you come to that conclusion?" Her brow furrowed.

"You had to be there. He's not necessarily evil. His convictions are sound." He leaned forward. "There's something else. I can't quite put my finger on."

"What is it?"

"I get the feeling I should know him."

"Say what?" Lynmore staggered back. "From where?

Your circle is limited to much of the White House and the surrounding area. And, outside of that, family."

"Exactly."

"He works for us?" Her eyes went wide. "For me?" She exclaimed.

The others in the room shifted nervously where they stood. She got really close to him and bent down.

"I want this kept quiet, you understand?" Her voice was low, barely a whisper. He nodded, not looking at her. "Barring some unforeseen monkey wrench, we handle it inside." She turned to her advisors and the secret service agents. In a normal voice, she said, "Are we clear?" Her bared teeth were enough to make them all nod. "Good."

The operative made his way through the prison corridor leading to Winters's cell. He had been placed in Palmers over a year ago as a precaution in case the plan took a wrong turn. In his hands, he carried a late snack. Orders were to keep the prisoner amicable. He snorted. Winters probably didn't know what that entailed.

"You fucking monster."

He turned the corner and headed down until he reached his destination. Winters was in a meditative position on the bed, as usual. The operative was certain it had nothing to do with centering or peace.

Probably thinking about how many he could kill before this is over.

Raising his keycard on the scanner, he waited for the click and entered. He set the tray next to Winters on the bed and stepped back.

"Daylight is a healthy part of a human's regimen," Winters spoke.

The operative made a confused face for the cameras and pointed to the snack.

"You need to eat that, or I'll get in trouble. And no,

it's not laced with anything. I prepared it myself." He turned to leave. "I'll be back for the tray in an hour."

Winters' eyes opened, and he got to see those infamous grey eyes. It was true. He made a person's insides feel like they were being iced over.

"A fallen empire needs no shadows," Winters added.

The operative frowned, exiting the cell. Winters made a habit of saying cryptic things to random soldiers. They weren't to him. He knew his real boss' orders from those two phrases. It was going to be a media shit storm.

⌒

Munston stared at the news feeds scrolling across the vidscreen in the role call room at the precinct. The other officers sat slack jawed, the chief standing at the front with a scowl. Next to him was the Mayor, equally upset. Every news outlet was on the story with fervor.

The list of the murder suspects names had been brought to the light of day. Press camping outside waited patiently for someone to come out and give them a sound bite. They would have to keep holding their breath.

"So, here's the kicker, ladies and gents," the chief announced. "An anonymous message was sent with locations of every suspect still alive. Apparently, a few of them were mysteriously dispatched."

"I don't have to tell you; the higher ups are livid. We do this discreetly, as best we can," the Mayor said. "We bring them in alive."

"Good to know," an officer laughed.

The chief and the Mayor turned to him angrily.

"Not a scratch on them or you lose your badge. Clear?" The Mayor asked.

He waited for acknowledgement. When every officer nodded their head, he appeared satisfied.

"Okay, everybody, get to it!" The chief ordered.

As the room dispersed, Munston lagged behind. The chief and Mayor finally noticed him and stopped their hushed discussion.

"What is it, detective?" The chief asked.

"Landers." He watched the chief go pale. "I'm sure you saw his name on that list."

The Mayor stepped to him and bent slightly to whisper in his ear.

"What part of discreetly don't you understand?"

"If anyone should go find him, it's me. I'll bring him in. To do that, I may have to go off the grid."

"Do what you have to do, detective. Just, remember what I said."

Munston stood and gave the chief a nod before heading out.

⌒

The head of the forensics team at Palmer raced to his car in the parking garage and got in. He still had his lab coat on. In his hand was his government issue secured tablet. He tossed it on the passenger seat and threw the car into reverse, out of the space. Minding his speed, he made it to the main gate in a semi calm manner. The time on the dash showed he had under two hours to make his meeting with the President. It took an hour and a half easy with no traffic. He had to get through security and be escorted to the Oval office. It was going to be tight.

Arriving at the White House checkpoint, he was whisked away by secret service agents and rushed through protocol. At the door of the Oval office, he brushed off his shirt while holding the tablet. The door swung open and he entered.

"Thomason, at your request, Madam President," the officer announced him.

"Good, leave us," she replied, sitting back at her desk.

There were six people in all, himself included, and the atmosphere was tense.

"What have you got for us?" She asked.

He scanned the faces in the room.

Oh boy!

"I was finally able to get more information on Winters."

"And?" Everyone seemed impatiently.

"He had a procedure done years ago. Age reversal. It's a very delicate and dangerous technique only a handful of scientists know how to do correctly."

"So, he's older than he looks. Fascinating, but what does that tell me?"

Thomason opened his tablet and brought up the file image of a middle-aged man with crow's feet and slight grey at the temples.

"This is what he originally looked like and his real name. I matched the DNA sample."

He turned it around and the Secretary of Homeland Security jumped from the loveseat. The President squinted at the picture, unsure.

"Who is he?" She turned to the Homeland Secretary

"That's the assistant to the Secretary of the Census Bureau!"

"What did you say?" She yelled.

The Vice President smacked a hand to his face and let it slide down. The Press Secretary slumped into a nearby chair. President Lynmore stood and came around her desk, wagging a finger as she approached him.

"No, no, no! Damn it, are you sure?"

"Yes, Madam President."

"There's no mistake?"

"None."

The Homeland Secretary got up to stretch and paced in a circle, deep in thought. He stopped.

"Winters knew who I was from the start. We met on

a few occasions some time ago. Not many people pay attention to the assistants in a department unless something big happens. He floated under the radar, probably doing his job remotely and no one the wiser."

A knock on the door interrupted their meeting and a page was let in.

"Sorry to barge in. Madam Press Secretary, it is out."

"What's out?"

"One of the President's cabinet members' employees is part of the murder ring."

She shot up from her seat.

"How?"

"Massive leak from an anonymous source. Law enforcement was blindsided too. The Mayor of the city is not taking this well."

Thomason's upper lip went inward as he stared at the President.

That's nothing. She's about livid. He said to himself.

"The good news is that no one knows who it is. His name has not been released or any images. Of course, that could change real fast."

The page attempted a smile.

"I want to talk him. Right now!" President Lynmore demanded.

"I don't think that's a good idea," the Vice President said. "It's obvious he knows how to play the game better than us. Don't set yourself up for a coup."

"What I supposed to do then?"

"Let me handle it," The Homeland Secretary answered.

⌐

Within days, the suspects were ushered under tight security and flashing press cameras into the jailhouse. An angry mob had been barricaded across the street to keep them at bay. The largest cell inside had been designated for the suspects as a precaution and to segregate them from other prisoners. The Police Chief paced his office with both hands on his hips as he watched the entourage of murderers being brought in. One of them, Emerson, if he remembered correctly, locked eyes with him. There was no malice or surprise concerning his predicament.

Is this all part of the plan? The chief asked himself.

After they were all locked in, he went to see the animals in their cage. Smug faces all around made his anger rise again.

"Welcome back," he greeted them.

Emerson let out a small laugh.

"Thanks for inviting us again."

"Well this time we're gonna' make sure you stay for the long haul."

"Is that right? I look forward to seeing you try."

Heated arguments erupted on the loading dock at Palmer. The two heads of security, the warden, Thomason, and the Homeland Secretary stood in a circle debating Winters.

"We can't just keep him here when all of creation knows he exists. Him not showing up for sentencing with the rest would raise too many questions," one of the heads of security said.

"He's a major threat to humanity and the government! Anything could go wrong during transport!" The warden yelled.

"This is not up for discussion. The President went through every scenario and we would look corrupt as fuck if we hid him. Transparency is key." George stated.

"Jesus! How are we getting him to the jail, let alone the courthouse?" The second security head asked.

"You act like he's going to try and escape and slaughter everyone." Thomason accused.

"Yes!" The warden replied. "I think he would."

George pinched his nose and let out a sigh. The other men didn't understand that Winters' employer already had a plan in motion. He had a sneaking suspicion the leaks came from him. A round up of all the players for the public to see.

"Ready him for transport," he ordered. "The quicker we get this done, the closer we get to an answer."

Winters let the guards unlock the shackles on his wrist and help him stand. Slip on shoes were set at his feet and he put them on while zip ties reconnected his wrists. He never took his gaze off the Homeland Secretary who waited in the corridor.

"You did this, didn't you?" George asked him. "Or, at the least, initiated it somehow."

The sides of his lips twitched upwards a bit.

"Did I?"

"You're going to talk to me now?" George seemed surprised.

"No. Not without my lawyer present."

"You're lucky we let you out to have a lawyer, you freak!" One of the head officers spat.

"It's a long drive." George said, giving the officer a dirty look.

"Silence is a virtue," Winters replied.

The entire entourage marched down the corridor, with Winters in the center, and out to the transport van waiting on the dock. He was secured to the floor by a thick rubber bar with reinforced metal latches on each end. George decided to ride in back with him. As the man climbed in, the doors were shut. A hand slapped twice on the side, signaling the driver to move out. They traveled in silence as promised, Winters observing George keeping a constant vigil on him.

A sea of press covered the front steps of the jail as they drove near. The van circumvented the fray and went to the back of the building. Winters smiled. It wasn't that easy. To the dismay of the guards, a smaller group of press were lying in wait, arguing with the officers blocking their path. He was unlatched and led by the elbow into the steel double doors. Mix matched words and flashing cameras bombarded the parade.

Inside, the chief's face was flustered to a hot pink. He got right in Winters's face and scrutinized him up and down. When he stared into his eyes, the chief flinched and backed away.

"Don't like what you see?" Winters asked softly, leaning towards him.

One of the prison officers yanked him back. He gave him a side glance and the man placed a hand on his weapon. Winters chuckled and stared at the chief.

"We have a communal cell for these monsters."

"He must be segregated," Thomason said.

"We don't have the resources for that!" The chief walked away then came back. "He goes in with the others, so we can keep an eye on all of them." He looked at The Homeland Secretary. "And you. Are you really staying here for arraignments?"

"Among other things, yes. This is a matter of national security. That being said, we will not interfere with your work."

"Until it suits your needs," the chief said.

Winters was escorted to the cell and his captured associates all turned to him in mock surprise. He was going to enjoy the game. For now.

Reporters caused a bottle neck in the halls of the judicial courthouse as they fought to get a spot inside for a glimpse of the alleged murderers. They had already been ushered in from the jail side, so the only option was to wait for someone to open the courtroom doors. News of the Grid Community and the atrocities within had been leaked around the world. The U.S. government decided it was time to intervene and that didn't bode well for the Shadow Organization. Even in the background of the purge, it could potentially expose them.

Neil Shannon sat in the back of the courtroom and waited for it to fill up. Up front were nine apprehended assassins, along with three government agents, and Winters sitting at one table with six lawyers surrounding them. The organization had a handful of court appointees on their roster and called in the favors. Each one had been top of their class and seasoned litigators. The prosecutors were going to meet their match during trial.

Winters seemed to be doodling on a note pad. He then moved it sideways into his line of sight and Neil saw the coded message. The public had no idea who Winters was aside from being involved with the killers and once revealed would send every politician into a frenzy. He thanked the heavens for it being a closed hearing.

Only a few networks were granted access and they brought their full gear, lights and all. Of course, that would not last long. As the sessions gain traction, it would open to the public and unleash chaos. Today was jury selection. Both sides were going to have a hell of a time finding peers for the accused. He sat back to enjoy the show.

When the judge entered, he rolled his eyes in disgust while rising per protocol. The man was known to be an asshole who didn't bend much to threats. A real man of justice with a ton of dirt kept hidden in his closet. There were a few operatives in town Neil could contact to get the ball rolling. He had no intentions of letting the proceedings be steered by that man.

I'll get him, Neil vowed to himself.

The Judge's luck was about to run out.

True to Neil's predictions, three weeks into the trial, the whole ordeal was being broadcast on national television and streamed around the world. So far, nothing was out of the ordinary. The prosecution brought in expert testimony regarding the methods of how each victim was killed and a lot of forensics. When it came to the murder of a Sector leader, the mood turned sour.

"Prosecution rests."

"Cross examine?" The judge asked. He didn't look up from his notes.

"Absolutely," one of the defendant's attorneys replied. He jumped up from his seat and made his way to the front of the room.

"So, tell me, what motives would any of my clients have against the deceased?"

"He was a prominent figure in the community. Some would be jealous of his success."

"Really? He had no ill deeds in his repertoire?" The lawyer asked snarkily.

"What are you implying?" The witness's expression grew dark.

"No dark secrets?"

"I'm not sure what you're…"

"Maybe running an underworld child sex ring for profit with his son, perhaps?"

Gasps erupted as the witness gripped the edge of the stand and leaned forward.

"How dare you?" He shouted.

The gavel came down three times and while the noise

rose instead of ceased, the judge pointed at the lawyer.

"I will not have you victim shame the dead nor the reputation of a distinguished pillar of society!"

"I'm only trying to establish their reasoning for my clients' motives." He smiled sweetly.

"That is not what you are doing. This is a smear tactic and I will not stand for it!"

"Is that because you identify with the deceased?"

"What did you say?" The judge's face went red.

The lawyer went to the table and picked up his tablet.

"May I approach the bench?" He didn't wait for permission. The tablet was set in front of the judge. "Please, hit the play icon." The judge complied.

"What is going on?" The head prosecutor demanded. "Is that evidence? Are you trying to blackmail the judge?"

"So many questions," the lawyer laughed. "The answer is no. I would never do such a thing." He turned back to the judge. "Isn't that so, your honor?"

Pale and noticeably in turmoil, the judge handed back the tablet. He cleared his throat.

"We will recess for thirty minutes." His voice shook as he banged the gavel and left.

The lawyer looked over at Neil in the back row and winked. Neil gave a nod back.

"What was that?" one of the other lawyers whispered.

"Oh, just a video of him going into a shady child sex establishment in the Grid City and getting his kicks on. He likes them a bit too prepubescent for my tastes."

"We have a dirty judge?" The lawyer on the end was incredulous, his eyes wide in disgust.

"That shouldn't surprise any of you," Emerson said.

"I'd like to think there was some sense of moral code in our justice department."

"Well, you're asking way too much," their other colleague stated.

Winters was scheduled to testify, and he had gotten word that the White House was ready to release a statement distancing themselves from him. He expected no less from the President and her subordinates. Neil and George sat incognito with the masses.

For a defendant to testify on their behalf was never recommended, yet he had insisted. Emerson expressed suspicion when he argued about it with one of the lawyers. He didn't explain his agenda to anyone. It was all part of the set up leading to his next plan.

Wearing an expensive smoky grey suit and tie that accented his steel, icy eyes, he straightened his jacket and stood when the bailiff called his name. A hush fell over the courtroom as he walked to the stand. The jury followed him with their eyes, some of them full of anger.

"Please raise your right hand." He smiled and obeyed. "Do you swear to tell the whole truth, and nothing more so help you and the one you deem most high?"

"I do," Winters cheerfully answered.

He sat down and waited for his lawyer to come forward.

"Please state your full name."

"Jeremiah Winters."

"Is that your real name?"

"Of course not."

"Please state your true name for the records."

"Joseph Winthrop."

George winced, bracing for what came next.

"And your occupation?"

"I am the assistant to the Secretary of the Census Bureau for the United States of America."

The courtroom went into an uproar. The Judge's expression changed from boredom to awe, then rage.

He repeatedly banged his gavel, shouting, "Order!" to

no avail. A din of voices echoed throughout while some newscasters ran out of the room to get in their sound bites. Which was their mistake.

"Seal it!" The judge ordered. "Close the doors and guard them!"

The people outside realized too late what was happening as they clambered to try and get back in before they were shut out. As the doors slammed, the courtroom fell silent again.

"What is the meaning of this?" The judge yelled. "Did you think you could cause a circus in my court and get away with it?" He addressed the lawyer.

"Not at all, your honor."

"Is this true?" The judge turned to Winters. "You work for the office of the President?"

"That is correct."

The other defendants stared at him in shock. Emerson was visibly angry.

"Get that jury out of here, now! I want them moved to a new location and briefed. We're taking a five-minute recess. No one leaves this room!"

He banged his gavel and headed back to his chambers.

"Well, that went," the lawyer said, "fucking all wrong!"

He slapped the notepad on the table across the room and went to lean on the table. Winters pulled on his shirt cuffs, making sure they were even. The prosecutors appeared shaken and frantically going through their notes. One of them glared up at Winters. As did the departing jury.

The judge came back and pointed to the lawyers.

"You better explain this," he yelled.

George stood and walked to the front. The judge's eyes went wide, and his teeth clenched. The man was on the verge of fury.

"My apologies, your honor. We thought it best not to

divulge some information. It never occurred to us that Mr. Winthrop would voluntarily expose himself."

"And what am I supposed to do now? He can't be tried in my court. You set me up!"

George moved closer to him and said softly, "You did that to yourself, being a regular patron at one of those damn establishments." He stepped back.

"Should we declare a mistrial," one of the lawyers asked.

"Over my rotting corpse!" The head prosecutor was up from his seat and pissed off. "I don't know what game you're playing, but those murderers are not going free on my watch."

"We will not separate our clients. Either try them as one or we move for the judge to be reassigned."

"You wouldn't dare," the judge seethed.

"Try and see," the lawyer on the end said.

All the color drained from the judge's face and he stood defeated. The prosecutors looked at each other in confusion. They finally figured it out and turned to the defendant table with dismay. The Judge ran a hand down his face and scanned the room. There were a few court reporters and a scattered number of spectators.

"The defendants will be sequestered until further notice. The prosecution has thirty days to come up with a new set of indictments."

He walked up to his podium, grabbed the gavel and banged it once before leaving.

"What?" The head prosecutor went to go after him. "This is bullshit! Your honor!"

The guards blocked his path while his colleague pulled him back by the arm. He turned to the Homeland Secretary, saliva forming on his lips.

"You government prick."

"Careful. You know who I am?"

He wiped his mouth with his jacket sleeve and stopped his advance.

George nodded to the line of guards filing in.

"Take the prisoners to their holding cell."

They all let themselves be restrained, even Winters didn't make a scene. The courtroom was cleared except for the lawyers and George. He took out his phone and made a call.

"Take them out. Not one should be conscious when I get there."

He hung up and made his way out to the hall. News crews had set up shop and the ones privy to the scene inside were already putting a spin on it. He passed by a female court reporter poised in front of her cameraman with the light shining on her.

"After the shocking revelation, the judge made an unprecedented move by having the alleged killers sequestered to an undisclosed location. We are getting word from the White House condemning Mr. Winters's, or rather, Mr. Winthrop's involvement in the murders."

The group of jailers and their wards walked down the corridor single file. They came to the communal cell and were shoved in.

"Hey! You need to take these off," Brent called out.

The jailers back up against the wall to make way for a second wave of uniformed guards armed with what looked like assault rifles. As some threw their hands up in protest and others tried to dodge as a storm of needles filled the cell. One by one, the agents dropped like dead weight.

One of the armed guards tapped the commlink in his ear.

"This is serpent. We are a go."

The cell was opened, and the unconscious agents were hauled off through the back door where a transport wagon waited.

MISSION COMPLETE

Winters woke gasping for air in a dark concrete cell almost the width of his height. He found out how accurate his calculations were when he turned in the bed and his feet nearly touched the wall. His vision adjusted to the dark and he found it was not the same wing as before. He was sure of his location.

Palmer.

The facility had different wings for certain types of prisoners. Since putting the entire group in the secret sector would raise to many questions, they had been put in maximum security. He could hear movement around him, confirming the cluster.

Easy access to each other.

The overhead lights in the cells flickered to life and shined dimly down on them. Not fully acclimated to their surroundings, many shielded their eyes. Winters got to see who was where. Directly across from him, Emerson sat up and held the side of his head.

"That was some nasty stuff."

"I say we were out for a couple of days," Winters said.

"Sons of bitches," Dowans muttered from his cell.

They had been paired up except for Emerson, Hammond, and himself and he wondered why. Footsteps echoed from farther down the corridor and he knew he was about to get his answer.

The head officer of the prison came into view at the center of the cluster. He grinned ear to ear and stepped towards Winters's cell.

"Thought you were clever, didn't you? Having your people take off with the bodies." Winters tensed. "We found them. Not the girl, but that will be soon. We're on it." He saw the confused looks from the others and held two fingers to his mouth as it made an O. "Did he not tell you what happened? Wait, I have a present for you." He pulled out his tablet and brought up a video. Using the projector function, he aimed it against the nearest wall so they could all see. "I watch it all the time. Makes me feel all warm and fuzzy inside."

On the wall was the entire safe house incident, from start to finish. Emerson fought back tears of rage as he watched Garrison being shot full of holes and Niles completely falling into insanity. The officer delighted in the rest trying to desperately contain their rage. When it was over, he shut down his tablet and put it away.

"We'll bring them down to join you in hell when our medical ward releases them. Whoever you sent them to did a damn good job of patching them up. They weren't completely healed when we hauled their asses here though."

He gave a shrug with both hands out.

The smile on his face was something evil. Winters vowed to kill him when he got the chance. He waited for the officer to slowly saunter back down the corridor, his guards in tow.

By the end of the week, Niles and Garrison were brought in on stretchers to the cell cluster. Both wore thin blue hospital scrubs with spots of blood where their wounds had opened from being jostled. Garrison was put in with Hammond and Niles with Winters. The guards weren't gentle with them either. Hammond was able to soften Garrison's landing on the bottom bunk by swinging down and position himself behind him as he fell back. Winters was pushed back out of the way as Niles was dumped like a meal sack. The guards snickered as they left, making jokes.

Winters made Niles as comfortable as he could, then climbed onto the top bunk. He assumed his meditation position and closed his eyes. He needed to clear his mind. Because at that moment, he was about to ruin all the progress he had made so far and kill everyone.

Each day, they were given three meals laced with sedatives and thirty minutes of fresh air on the deserted side of the compound. They wore prison issued blue scrubs with a serial number inked on the front and polyester drawstring booties. On their outdoor excursions, they donned slip on shoes and a sweater. The first two weeks, going outside was by preference since someone had to stay with Niles and Garrison. After that, Winters helped Niles around while Emerson took care of Garrison.

Winters observed how everyone interacted with each other, including the guards. He started to notice something odd about the way some of the other imprisoned agents reacted to their treatment so far. They weren't being grossly mistreated, yet complaints cropped up.

"Why are we being isolated?" Brent asked the head guard. "I'm pretty sure it looks bad that no one has seen us in a while."

"It's not your decision," the head guard said through closed teeth. "Until they say otherwise, we get to do whatever we want to you."

"I think, at some point, you guys are going to have to show us off in gen pop and let us eat real food."

"Not happening." The head guard shoved Brent back in line with the others. "Time for your daily outdoor adventure. You get a whole hour today."

Winters put Niles' arm around his shoulder and held him up. Still out of it, he was able to walk a little on his own. More of a shuffle. His eyes were empty of emotion.

"Bet on it," Brent muttered under his breath.

That made Winters perk up and stare at him for a moment. He sensed the same vibe coming from Dowans. Emerson readjusted Garrison's arm and let him lean closer for leverage.

"Let's move out, girlies!"

Six guards, two at the front, back and each side of them walked with taser sticks charged and ready. The head guard grinned, hoping to see them being used.

I'll kill you last, Winters said to him silently.

Within a few weeks, the head guard came into the cluster's center looking livid. He glared at Brent and clasped both hands behind him.

"There was an uproar regarding your disappearance. As such, the government has authorized for you to mingle with the general population and join in the chow hall. You will not be moved! This is your home. When you are not engaged in activities or eating, you are to report back here. Understood?" He scanned each cell. "Good." The cells locking mechanisms clicked. "Line up! Time for breakfast."

The cafeteria was jam packed with every walk of hardened criminals. From the moment the group of agents filed in, the other inmates stopped and turned to get a good look. They obviously knew who they were. Winters realized quickly that they were in a high security wing for civilian offenders. He wondered why it was necessary to be driven ten minutes away.

The inmates on this side wore short sleeved jumpers with stenciled numbers on the back.

A prisoner nearly seven feet tall and all muscle stepped up to Winters and looked down at Niles slumped against him. He turned his head and saw Emerson with Garrison.

"You guys supposed to be bad ass assassins?" He snorted. "Look like soft ass fucka's to me."

Winters looked up at him.

"Walk away."

The man smiled and cracked his knuckles. His face suddenly contorted, and he dropped to the floor convulsing. Two of their guards had the taser sticks pressed deep in the inmate's back. The head guard came up behind his group.

"Don't touch the merchandise."

The rest of the room went back to normal and the volume intensified as conversations resumed. Once the entire group was seated with their trays, the guards left them. Some of the other prisoners seemed to have been waiting for that. One came behind Niles while he slowly took tiny bites of food.

"This one's a bit too pretty. He should be bit more roughed up, don't you think?"

His hand grabbed a fistful of hair and he ran his fingers through it. Niles stopped eating, the spork midway to his lips. Another prisoner stood and walked over.

"Yeah, they all look a little too clean and pampered."

The regular prisoners didn't move or blink an eye. Instead, they seemed to find it amusing. That told Winters there would no help from them unless the situation got out of hand. And it was about to. He moved away from Niles as the two prisoners had a laugh. Dowans' eyes went wide, and Garrison shook his mouthing the word no.

Mid laugh, the first inmate's face went sideways and blood flew onto the other man next to him. While he was still disoriented from the unseen blow, Niles was up with his hand gripped behind the inmate's head. He smashed it into the head of the other. More blood went spewing onto the table as both men tumbled to the floor. The prison guards moved. Winters gave them a side glance. Too late.

Niles' eyes burned with animalistic rage and before he could cause anymore damage, Hammond tackled him down. A massive fight erupted throughout the cafeteria. Alarms went off and a male voice blasted through the PA system.

"This wing is now on lockdown. Guards, please restrain all prisoners and return them to their designated holding facility."

Emerson crawled under the table along with Winters.

"At least we got to eat half our food before all hell broke loose."

Winters' stare was venomous. He glanced over at Hammond still holding down Niles who had already relented and lay still.

"We shouldn't be here," he said.

"Well, whatever happened to bring this about, we have to go with it."

A guard grabbed Emerson by the leg and he was drug out. Despite not resisting, the guard hit him in the head with a billy club.

"Aww, this is bullshit!"

He shielded himself from the pummeling while another guard attached ankle cuffs to his wrists and hauled him up like cattle. Winters was being trussed up as well, his demeanor calm.

~

Winters walked down the corridor leading to the laundry room. He pushed the rickety cart with one hand and kept a leisurely pace. His group had been in Palmer over two months and still no word from their lawyers or any government officials regarding the new trial. Over the course of their stay in new surroundings, he observed everything and everyone. He saw how the guards operated, what the inmates did on the side in their free time, and interactions.

As he neared the first entrance of the laundry room, he caught a glimpse of Brent and an inmate conversing in low voices by the washer. He recognized the prisoner as a contact for the outside who also brought their meals once a week when they were confined on the other side. Winters continued his walk to the second entrance, not stopping.

He was scheduled to work in the cafeteria two days later and while moving the giant pots off the rack, he saw the same prisoner talking up the head cook, pointing to the menu board for next week. Winters scanned the list, memorizing it. He wasn't sure of its significance. Better safe than sorry.

Another fight broke out during lunch in the cafeteria the following week and this time, Addams was the culprit, antagonizing a prisoner twice his size. In the throes of the melee, Winters watched how Brent's eyes darted around searching. The guards from their wing came to retrieve them and they were on lockdown in the cluster once more. Later in the day, the head guard made an appearance.

"It seems, you all are not welcomed back for the rest of the day, so dinner will be served here. They're not total dicks, though. The cafeteria has prepared a fine meal. A crew is delivering it."

Winters made a mental note of the day and remembered what was to be served. It came to no surprise when he saw the contact prisoner as one of the delivery boys. He glanced at the contents on the plastic wrapped trays and understood. That dish was not on the menu.

"Cook made this special since you all aren't really part of gen pop," the first delivery guy said. "Guess, you guys need more attention." He smirked. The head guard gave him a sharp look and it disappeared.

"Get to it!"

"Whatever," the prisoner said softly.

The food was issued out to each cell and the delivery men hurried out with their empty carts.

Niles sat staring at the tray of food Winters set in front of him and finally lifted the spoon. Winters grabbed his wrist as he scooped up an edge of the pasta.

"Let go," Niles said in a hushed voice dripping with malice.

"I know you don't want to be in the same room with me," he said, tightening his grip. "You have to deal with it and listen to me." Niles pulled harder and Winters finally released him. "We're all going to get sick after we eat this!" Winters seethed. He watched Brent hesitating before taking a bite. "Some more than others."

"What are you talking about?" Niles eyes opened wider and he tried to push the tray away. Winters stopped him. "What are you doing? I'm not eating that!"

"Yes, you are," Winters replied angrily. "We don't want to cause an uproar and we have handled worse things than poison."

Winters took in Niles' appearance. Dark circles lay heavy under dark lifeless eyes, his skin was slightly jaundiced, and there was a slight shake in his hands. He hadn't fully recovered, and the poison would do him in fast.

The other worry was Garrison.
Damn it!

"Eat! We don't have much time before they come for the trays."

Niles glared at him then at the food. Reluctantly, he raised the spoon and took the first taste of the tainted meal.

Within an hour, everyone in the group was sick. Some had intense cramps, others began violently throwing up. Addams, Brent, Garrison, and Niles started convulsing. The head guard came running in, furious.

"What the fuck is going on!" He demanded from the guards standing in the center of the cluster not sure what to do.

"Not sure. I think it's," the guard's expression became shock as he turned to his boss. "I think it's food poisoning."

The head guard's body went rigid and he scanned each cell.

"Those sons of bitches," he muttered. "Get them all to medical! And make sure it is secured. I don't want any more surprises." He turned to leave.

"Where are you going, boss?"

"To have a chat with the kitchen staff in gen pop."

As he left, one of the guards hit the emergency call button.

Somewhat recovered, Winters sat up in his hospital bed and took stock of the medical wing. The equipment was state of the art and the staff was hostile. He watched Brent feign a better condition than he was and try to convince the nurse to release him. A few of the group had already been sent back with stomach medicine. When she finally agreed, Winters decided to do the same. He donned his blue scrubs and booties, tossing the medical gown at the foot of the bed.

Brent dressed in record speed and waited for the guard to tie his wrists.

"I have laundry duty today. You guys going to escort me there, right?"

"Yeah, whatever." The restraints secured, the guard grabbed him under the arm. "Let's go."

A guard came for Winters

"Let me guess, you got duty as well?"

"That is correct," Winters replied. "I would appreciate your escort service."

"Don't get uppity with me, you monster."

He strapped on the ties and roughly hauled Winters out of the infirmary.

Luckily, Brent and his guard were a decent distance ahead, giving Winters time to see where he would go once untied. After both men reported to the laundry room, Brent went off to the other side where the clean beddings were stored. Winters followed like a second shadow, the other agent not noticing his tail. Inside, Brent reached under a high pile of sheets and pulled out a tablet. A handwritten post it note with the login credentials was stuck to it. Winters observed him for a while as he accessed the device and began reading.

Voices from the hallway made Brent stop and shut down the tablet. He shoved it back under the sheets and went out the second doorway. Winters eased away from his position by the main door and walked back to the laundry room.

The sparsely furnished cells and lack of light would make most humans depressed after so long. Winters laid in bed, hands behind his head, staring at the ceiling, imagining it caving in from rot. Only problem, there was no rot. Palmer was pristine. He heard the locks engage on the cell door signaling lights out in ten minutes.

The cluster would be engulfed in darkness. He waited an hour afterwards to flip down and land silently on Niles' bunk.

A spark of light flashed in his eyes and his vision corrected, enabling him to see in the pitch dark. He reached under the mattress and pulled out the mini syringe he had swiped from medical. It contained a mild sedative yet strong enough to sap half the strength of a wild animal. With a quick jab while pushing the injector button, he administered the drug. The needle was so tiny, Niles didn't feel it.

Winters pulled the blanket off him and positioned one hand on the left side of Niles' ribcage. He moved slowly down and finding the spot where a pressure point cylinder would be, pushed hard. That woke Niles up. He held fast to his side as Niles attempted to deliver a palm punch under his chin. Winters dodged it and used his other hand to clamp down on Niles mouth. He saw the circle of blue light in his eyes and pressed harder. Niles struggled beneath him even as his body finally started to shift. Tears streamed down from the corners of his eyes.

"I'm sorry," Winters whispered as he pushed the top of his pants down past his thighs. "This is the only thing I can give you."

He released his hold on the pressure point and removed Niles' pants in one motion. As he leaned forward, spreading Niles legs around his waist, he could see the sedative take effect. Niles' body relaxed a bit and he was able to force his way in with minimal effort. A sharp pitch escaped from Niles through his fingers.

"Shhh. I won't take long."

With each thrust, he felt Niles try to tense up only to have her body not obey, eyes squeezed shut as she endured the pain Winters gave. He was never one of those gentle, love making types. He did the best he could in this situation. Niles's walls tightened around him and she again tried to punch and push him off.

"That's it, take it," he whispered.

A small whimper came as her body arched upwards. Winters gritted his teeth, stifling an outburst as his seed flowed into her. When he finished, Niles' body slumped down into the bed like dead weight, her head flopped sideways. He checked her pulse and felt it slow down to a crawl. She was unconscious and would be for a while, possibly days.

Winters put the scrub pants back on her and pulled the blanket all the way up. He pulled his own up and climbed back to his bunk. The first stage of his agenda accomplished, he sat with his head against the wall and gathered his thoughts.

Now. My purge begins.

The tablet was still in the hiding spot when Winters reported for laundry duty. He donned a pair of nitrile gloves and pulled it out, accessing it per the note's instructions. A document appeared, and he read who it came from. Not from one of their lawyers, instead a prosecutor. The file contained a deal that covered Addams and Brent. It sent the rest of them to death row for the gas chamber or lethal injection. He couldn't believe that was still going on in their new era of evolution. A notation on the last page caught his eye.

Oh? So, that's it.

Winters shut it down, replaced the note and shoved the tablet back in the sheet stack. He snapped the gloves off and grabbed a large pile of towels for his cart. A slow burn developed in his mind.

Towards the end of the shift, Winters went back through and found Brent reading the second part of the document asking for confirmation in agreement of the terms. Winters stood in the doorway behind him and waited. Brent's shoulders jerked, and he stood still.

"You really are a dangerous man," he said to Winters.

"Yet, you know this and plan to try and get rid of me with that."

Brent turned around with an expression of rage.

"I am not trading my life or freedom for the rest of you!"

"That's too bad. We are all one team." He snapped one of the gloves he was wearing.

"Fuck that! I guess, I'll get rid of you first."

Brent came at him, a crudely made shiv in his hand and Winters managed to lean sideways. It sliced through the air millimeters from his cheek. He grabbed hold of Brent's forearm and flipped him down to the ground. Brent used his legs to bring Winters down with a swift kick to his calves. He rolled over and retrieved the shiv, bringing it down towards Winters's face. Winters stopped it inches from his eye and brought his knee up, hitting Brent in the scrotum. Not fazed, Brent pushed down harder. The blow had changed his leverage and Winters took advantage, twisting his wrists until Brent's grip loosened. He head butted him and rolled from beneath.

As both men stood up, the outside contact prisoner came running into the narrow room.

"Hey, Brent. What the hell is going on?"

Winters got hold of Brent's head and snapped it sideways. His body spun around and dropped to the floor. The contact's face formed in shock and before he could turn to leave, Winters had him by the neck. He dragged the man further in.

"Whatever you got paid, wasn't enough," Winters sneered.

He used one of Brent's signature moves that snapped the spine and neck. When the man's bod went limp, he took a towel and wrapped the man's hand around the makeshift knife. He made three stabs in quick succession in the same area on Brent's abdomen and waited for enough blood to pool on the shirt. Then he dragged the body to the laundry shoot and tossed it in.

The contact's body he dumped into one of the cloth lined push carts and piled some more dirty laundry on top. He peeked out into the hall and confirmed no one else was around. The contact had made sure Brent would be undisturbed. Winters walked down to the boiler room entrance and tossed his gloves into the incinerator shoot.

One down.

Back at the cluster, the guards were arguing. One of them pointed towards his and Niles's cell while another kept tapping his tablet that listed the roster.

"That one hasn't come off his bunk since last night and it's the end of the day again."

"Who cares?" the other yelled. "We got one of those fuckers missing. How are we supposed to explain this to the bossman?"

"How indeed." The head guard stepped into the center and the two men became gripped with fear. "Which one?"

"Huh?" The first guard blinked.

"Who is missing?"

"Brent, sir. He never reported back from his duties in the east wing."

Winters saw Addams tense up in his cell.

The head guard moved to the cell where Niles lay still unconscious and stood before it.

"Open it."

The lock disengaged, and Winters felt his stomach drop. This could go either way. The head guard walked in and stared down at Niles for what seemed like minutes. He then turned to Winters, his eyes like daggers.

"Is this your doing?" He stepped back. "Of course it is. Who else would have access besides my guards? And I know you would never allow such a thing."

"You're right." Winters gave him a sly smile.

"Call medical and have this one removed from this wing." He left the cell, passing Winters. "Once cleared, put Niles in solitary confinement."

"You can't move her," Winters started to argue. "She could…"

The head guard turned back around and got close to him.

"You should have thought of that beforehand. I don't give a damn what happens to either one of you."

From across the way, Emerson's expression was one of disbelief. Dowans gave Winters a look of disgust. Winters locked eyes with the head guard.

"If anything happens to Niles, you're going to have a bigger problem."

The head guard snorted and walked off. A medical unit came with a stretcher and parked it by the cell. They went in and lifted Niles off the bunk. A strangled cry was heard, and Niles was brought out to be dropped on the stretcher. One of the guards came near them, tablet in hand.

"Hmph. Guess this one is pretty enough to tap, huh?" He called out to his colleague. "We should go down to solitary later and get some."

The other guard came up next to him and taking a peek at Niles, nodded.

"Sounds good to me." He grabbed a few strands of Niles hair and let them fall from his hingers.

"You touch her," Winters said. "And I will gut you like a pig and rip out both your intestines." Both men froze as they stared into his grey eyes glinting like starlight. The medical team, also frightened, undid the wheel locks on the stretcher and hauled out of the cluster. The guards were still rooted in place when Winters went into his cell and climbed up onto his bunk.

As the group was let loose out in the open for their daily one hour recess, Emerson grabbed Winters by the front of his shirt and slammed him into the side of the building.

"How could you? What the hell is wrong with you?"

"I don't have to explain anything to you."

"Oh, yes you do! Niles has been through enough shit and didn't need this."

Winters pushed him off and Emerson came right back, his hand around Winters's neck.

"Where's Brent? 'Cause last time I checked, you were both on laundry duty together." Winters stared at him knowingly and Emerson went pale. "Why?"

"He tried to kill me first."

While Emerson looked up, stunned, Winters smacked his hand away and headed towards the far end of the yard. On the other side, Addams appeared nervous, and angry. Dowans was deep in thought at one of the picnic benches. Emerson suddenly felt a chill in the air.

What am I missing?

The next day, during the early hours of dawn, Addams was found at the wing's main entrance fried to a crisp. His skin was charred black in perfect lines from the laser grid. Two other prisoners were with him, signifying an attempted prison break. A guard and wing manager were being hauled to the warden's office as accomplices.

Emerson sat in his cell trying to figure out why Addams would have set up such an operation and not tell any of them. He looked over at Winters sitting quietly in his cell not surprised at all by the turn of events. The others in the group were avoiding him like a plague, and it fit his current demeanor. Emerson had no doubt, Winters was about to rack up a body count and for all he knew, could be next.

Their entire wing was on lockdown for three days which meant he would have to wait for a chance to reach his own contact within the prison. Something wasn't right. He glanced over in the cell that housed Garrison and Hammond. The way Hammond appeared to keep his distance from Garrison was now, not only odd, but suspicious.

What the hell is going on?

He finally got to find out for himself on the third day after lockdown when his contact slipped him a note during lunch. He read the instructions and ate the note. Winters raised his eyebrows at him from across the table. When he was done eating, he followed the rest of the prisoners to the free activity sector and headed for the library. There was a keycard waiting for him in one of the books on the shelf. He made his way to the upper levels and touched the keycard to an office wing.

There was no staff present. He went further down and used the keycard again to enter a small closet next to an office. A listening device was set up and he inserted the earbuds. He could clearly hear the recorded conversation from the office.

"We found this tablet in the laundry room. Seems like someone was desperate for outside contact." A man's voice said.

"What's on it?" The second male voice asked.

"No idea. Thing is busted up pretty good. We got our forensics department on it."

"And the bodies?"

"We're not going to tell anyone shit about that!"

"It's obvious, the two prisoners were conspiring with

each other. One happened to get greedy it seems."

"It always amazes me how many weapons these animals can make with close to nothing."

There was a knock followed by the sound of a door lock clicking.

"What did you find out?"

The third person let out a long breath.

"Looks like a legal document." The voice was distinctively female. "Most of it was corrupted but we got enough to figure it out."

"And?"

"The deal was for Brent and Addams. Both would get immunity and a payout."

"What about the others?"

"Nothing. Guess they were getting hung out to dry."

Emerson squeezed his eyes shut, curbing the rage building inside him. He felt his mouth tighten as his teeth clenched. He began to rock aback and forth. Taking a few deep breaths, he managed to call himself again. Regardless of the plan, he felt Winters didn't have to kill Brent. His head shot up and he realized what the office members said. Winters had made it look like the two men had fought, not him.

You clever monster.

He removed the earbuds and wiped them down with an alcohol wipe left by the device. He left the closet and retraced his steps until he came to the lower levels office entry. Once inside, he walked to the end of the hall where a communal shredder sat and dropped in the key-card. He could manage his way back into the recreation room without getting caught.

At dinner, Emerson purposely sat near Winters, slamming his tray down for effect. He had promised to give Winters a talk on behalf of the others. He sat on the bench and stared him down.

"That was not necessary," Emerson said. "You could have incapacitated him, make him see reason."

Winters shoved a forkful of meat in his mouth and chewed slowly, his gaze never wavering from Emerson's. When he was done, his fork drop.

"What reasoning do you think we could've agreed on?"

"I know what most of that deal entailed. Was it stupid on their part? Absolutely."

"Most of it?" Winters asked stoically.

That made Emerson sit up straight.

"Then what am I missing," he asked.

"The part where if we so happen to meet our demise in prison, they get a big chunk of money and new identities."

Emerson forced himself not to look surprised.

"That still doesn't justify what you did. Especially to Niles."

Winters's expression grew dark.

"That has nothing to do with the other."

"Then tell me what you know about why Dowans and Hammond are acting guilty."

"Because they are."

"Winters…"

"I'm just part of the remedy."

"You can't go around killing us all. I will stop you if I have to."

"I can, I won't kill everyone, and you can't."

Emerson leaned back as Winters picked up his fork and continued eating.

⌒

Winters waited for Dowans to finish his conversation with the dirty administrator who happened to be visiting Palmer on a routine visit. He didn't believe in timely coincidences when it came to the government. He watched the administrator's face scrunch up as Dowans became more animated. Both men suddenly looked around and Dowans was left alone standing in the deserted hallway.

"Negotiations not going so well?" Winters walked towards him.

Dowans turned to face him, visibly angry.

"You really think I'm going down with the ship? They have no intention of giving us due process. We are going to rot in here as government play things."

"Not true. There was always an exit strategy."

"Bullshit!"

"You have no faith in the organization?"

Dowans' eyes went wide. "Fuck the organization. If it wasn't for them, I wouldn't be here. And you," his face went pink. "I know damn well you were the one who told those guys it was the perfect time to make a jail break, ahead of their schedule. You might as well have killed Addams yourself."

Winters smiled.

"And I know Landers didn't tell you about Childs and Ilan," he said

He watched Dowans expression falter, the corners of his mouth starting to twitch. He too, left the man there to contemplate his fate. As he rounded the corner, he spotted Emerson flat against the wall, hands balled into fists.

"Still think I'm not justified?" He asked softly in passing.

The list, was all that went through Emerson's mind as he headed back to the cluster with the rest of the group. That goddamned list! He had heard about it while on the run. The agents who were somehow found and dragged out of hiding. Some only to be executed for sport. He spotted Dowans going into his cell and felt heat creep up to his face. If not for that list…" He watched as Garrison slowly laid down on his bunk, Hammond reluctantly helping him. Emerson climbed into his bed, closed his eyes, and regulated his breathing.

I'll just sleep on it.

Winters started a fight at breakfast. At first, Emerson thought nothing of it, this being the norm every couple of weeks. Then he saw, amid the whirlwind of bodies beating each other to bloody pulps despite the guards jumping in with taser rods, Winters dragging Dowans facedown to the floor and stab him in the back of the neck with the long end of the spork. He broke off the round edge and tossed it across the room. The only evidence of an entry wound was a small black mark.

Emerson lay on the floor in awe. Winters never looked his way. A guard got hold of him and he didn't resist. The fight finally died down and the circle of prisoners was broken. As they were dragged off, one by one, the inmates underneath were exposed. Two had broken necks, one was screaming, holding his dangling arm with the other, and Dowans. Out of the corner of his eye, he found Winters. Before the guard got his hands tied, he held up his fingers.

Three.

Time was not on Hammond's side. Emerson became well aware of that as he observed the man get more agitated by the day. Winters was a vulture circling his prey. Emerson decided to confront him in the showers. With no way to hide anything, he figured the man would fess up to his misdeeds. He waited until everyone in the group was wet and soaping up.

"Isn't there something you need to tell us, Hammond?"

Everyone turned to look at Emerson then him.

"What do you mean?"

"I don't like the way Dowans checked out, but he kind of deserved it, don't you think?"

This time, some of the others rinsed off and stepped away from the shower heads.

"What's he talking about?" Killian asked. Felps went to finish getting the rest the shampoo out of his hair and came back. "How would he deserve to die like a dog in this shithole?"

"Don't know what you mean," Hammond muttered.

"The list," was all Emerson said.

There was silence for a moment. Jansen stepped up to Hammond and stood inches from him.

"You wouldn't know about that, right?"

"Wait," Felps said. "What list?" Then it dawned on him. "You mean, that list?" He yelled.

The others gave him looks of disdain and he scanned the entrance to make sure the guards weren't coming.

"You son of bitch. Were you and Dowans working with each other?"

Hammond's face contorted into a sneer.

"None of this was supposed to happen! No, I wasn't working with Dowans. I just gave the information to the highest bidder. I guess it was the government and Dowans had made a deal."

Garrison, weary and barely able to stand planted his hands on the wall for leverage.

"Why?"

Hammond's expression crumbled, and he backed away from all of them.

"You should have just died like the rest of them. I didn't need to see you stumbling around as some reminder."

"That you're a traitor?" Winters added.

"I wish I could kill you right now," Emerson whispered.

"You can," Winters said. Hammond glared at him. "But I won't let you." He pushed Felps and Jansen out of the way before any of them could react and had Hammond by the throat. "I will," he seethed in Hammond's face.

The three government agents who kept silent all through it, moved and attacked Winters, forcing him to release his grip. Emerson stood stunned for a moment then realized something was off. Felps caught on and grabbing one of the assailants by the hair, flung him into the nearest wall. The impact sounded like a hard shell cracking followed by a streak of blood rinsed off from the still flowing showers. Hammond took the opportunity to put Killian in a head lock before he could assist Winters as well. To his surprise, Killian dropped down to the wet tile and threw him over. Hammond's body hit the two agents on top of Winters, knocking them off.

In the distance, they could hear the guards coming. While he was still down, Winters delivered a killing blow to his chest, crushing the ribcage and puncturing his heart. One of the rogue agents grabbed Emerson by the face and kneed him. Felps came behind him and snapped his neck. The second he fell dead on the floor, Jansen hit the third with a palm under the nose. The man's eyes rolled back in their sockets and he slumped against the wall before sliding down.

The guards came in ready to apprehend them but stopped as they turned, forming a line across. Stark naked and covered in blood, they dared the guards to try. The first guard tapped his taser rod, setting off a spark.

"Let's teach these animals how to behave in a cage."

The guards advanced.

"This will be lesson in pain, for you," Winters said.

The head guard marched towards the shower room with a combat unit in tow. He could hear fighting and the sounds of heavy objects hitting against something solid as he got closer. Busting open the doors, he came to a full-on scene of carnage. The last of the six guards in charge of the group was being put down by Emerson. Winters turned, wiping blood from his face and smiled at him.

"Come to join the festivities?"

"Kill every last one of them. I will divide my cut evenly to whoever's left standing," the head guard ordered.

"So, it really was true," Emerson said softly. "All for money?"

"Greed is a powerful thing," Felps said.

"Are we really going to have this debate now?" Garrison asked, nodding to the oncoming mob of raging soldiers.

They clashed together, reminiscent of an ancient battlefield inside the watery confines of the prison bathroom. The head guard came directly at Winters, baring his teeth.

"You monster! I should have got rid of you in the beginning."

Winters laughed, startling the man. His grey eyes flashed bright.

"I always wanted to save you for last."

Winters closed his fingers together and rammed his hand into the head guard's abdomen. The man looked down in shock as blood dripped from his mouth. The fighting stopped.

"Jesus Christ!" One of the soldiers exclaimed, retreating from the group.

The ones still standing did the same. Winters didn't take his eyes off the head guard even when his eyes glazed over in death. With his hand still inside him, Winters spoke.

"You will get me a meeting with the warden. And you are going to release Niles from solitary." He removed his hand, shoving the head guard's body away from him onto the carpeted edge by the benches. "Do you understand?"

One of the soldiers began speaking into his radio.

"Sir, we have a situation here."

Emerson stared at Winters. He couldn't fathom would kind of person could kill someone like that. He was no saint and had killed many. The way Winters did it, though, terrified even him. One good outcome in all that transpired; Winters was a former government cabinet member assistant who knew how to negotiate.

It wasn't what you would call a prison break, since the warden and a few guards personally escorted them out of the installation during the dead of night. Only four of the high beams were on to minimize flood of light. The tower guards were not at their posts. After four months of being locked up in secret, what was left of the suspected killers were jumping ship. Winters held on to a pregnant, half-conscious Niles as they made their way down the concrete stairs. Ahead of him were Emerson, Garrison, and Felps. Heading up the rear, were Jansen and Killian. They all took slow calculated steps, making as little noise as possible. Thin clouds covered most of the moon to give it an eerie glow. A chill lingered in the air despite it being mid-March.

In front of the gates sat an older seven seat minivan. The side doors were wide open, and Winters saw what could only be provisions crammed in the back. A guard tossed Emerson the fob and he caught it midair. He sat in the driver seat and pushed the start button. The engine quietly came to life along with the automatic lights.

The warden came up to the side of the vehicle as they all piled in. Winters gently laid Niles in the seat behind the front passenger and strapped her in. She let her head fall back against the seat and closed her eyes.

"I don't have to tell you to haul ass out of here," the warden said.

"Nope," Emerson replied while adjusting the seat.

"And I sure as shit don't need to know which way you're heading."

"Wouldn't tell you anyway."

"This is not my call. If it were up to me," the warden began.

"But it's not," Emerson interrupted.

"I would see you all rot in here." The warden gave them all a frown. "Regardless of it being orders from the top, you're all still a bunch of murderers."

"For God and Country," Garrison quipped.

The warden clinched his fists. Winters snorted at his righteous indignation. He had no idea what the government was up to yet had the audacity to judge them.

"And you," the warden turned to Winters. "You were a cabinet member for the President. What you did is treason."

"Are you done?" Winters stood and stared at him. The warden flinched. "Instead of you lecturing a bunch of highly skilled assassins, you should be making sure we are on our way."

The warden circled his finger in the air and two of the guards hit the gate release. It made a soft thud as the mechanism disengaged and the thick plexiglass eased open wide enough to let the van out. The side doors were slammed shut and Emerson drove off into the night. He could see the warden and the guards standing in a row watching them while the gate reversed motion and began to close.

Felps rummaged through the packs in the rear to see what they had for the long trip. Winters turned towards him.

"Well?"

Felps rose and twisted his body around.

"Lots of junk food, nonperishables, two cases of water and some blankets."

"Funds?"

Garrison held up a stack of prepaid cards he pulled from the glove box. A few of them were for gas, just in case. The vehicle was a hybrid. Winters relaxed in his seat and Felps climbed back into his.

"How long you think before anyone realizes we're gone or the warden opens his mouth?" Killian asked.

"If they do as they're told, a few days. We were all in solitary confinement for safety reasons and the only guards who had contact with us just let us go," Garrison answered.

"By then we should be safely in the spot," Jansen said.

"That's the plan."

Winters looked over at Niles. Pain etched on her face as she tried to get comfortable. He felt a tug of regret. None of this should have happened this way. He knew how corrupt certain factions within the government were and how deep it went. The scene from Niles's house replayed in his head and he fought it back into the recesses of his mind. There was no point in reliving that nightmare. He caught Emerson eyeing him in the rearview mirror.

Emerson slowed the car as it neared a large gate with the community name blazed on the plaque attached to it. He dug out the sensor from the armrest and aimed it at the box on the side of the stone wall. The gates swung open to a long road that curved out of sight to the right. Along the way, he noticed the well paved landscape. Five minutes later, the road opened to reveal a cluster of cul de sacs three times the usual size.

Three level houses lined the streets, all similar in construction like a suburbia hell. He pulled into the first one and parked the van at its edge. The center had a round area of greenery with benches and small tables. He smacked his passenger in the chest with the back of his hand. Awake, Felps looked up out the window and let out a slow, "Wow."

In the back, Winters stirred from his troubled slumber to also take a peek. The cookie cutter homes and brightness of the day made him frown.

"Looks like Niles is going to be a soccer mom in this joint," Felps snorted as he too sat up, wiping sleep from his eyes.

"It'll keep us hidden for a while," Winters said. He gently shook Niles and heard a soft whimper. "Come on, sweetheart. We're home."

"Never thought I would ever hear you say something so nice to another human being."

Garrison eased himself up and leaned forward until his head touched the back of the seat before him. He winced as his arm hung relaxed. The muscles were taunt as was the skin where the bullet wounds had been repaired. Palmer had nowhere near the medical technology as the facilities or Shadow headquarters. His injuries were taking a lot longer to heal than necessary.

"Let me guess, we're assigned one of these?" He asked Emerson.

"The info is on the tablet in the glove compartment."

Felps took it out and after booting it up, found the data.

"Well, Winters and Niles are registered as married in the third house over. You and Garrison are in the one across from it. Oh!" He tapped Emerson and pointed to a car in the driveway of the center house. They all sat up straighter. "Childs is registered to that one. With a wife, no less."

As Winters got out of the car, Childs came out of his house.

"You made it. We were getting a bit worried."

Winters stopped in his tracks. "We?"

Childs pointed to the first house on the end.

"Landers and Munston are in there. And Ilan is on that side." He swung his arm the opposite way. "So much to talk about."

"Yes. Like who your supposed wife is," Winters said. His grey eyes turned dark.

Childs became defensive and both men stood in a locked staring match.

"Seriously," Ilan yelled as he came out his front door. "After all we've been through, you two gonna' have a brawl in the courtyard?" They averted their gaze and stepped away from each other. "That's better." He walked up to Emerson as he exited the car and they slapped hands. "Good to see you. And you," he pointed to Garrison, "still alive."

"So, what's the new order?" Felps asked.

"There's a house in the other cul de sac with a communications room. We get our instructions from there."

"As long as there's no more killing for a bit," Emerson said.

"Yeah," Felps concurred. "I'm exhausted."

⌒

As the only two left inside to get the job done, the facility agents dressed in combat gear were lying on their bellies observing the monolith through wearable zooming lenses. They scanned the area looking for a way to get in from below. Their target was deep underground inside it. Three people lounged around in each corner; reading on a tablet, nursing a drink with small sips, pacing while on their phone. Watchers. Their demeanor let the two agents know they were not from the Shadow Organization or the Facilities Group. These were United States government operatives.

"What do you think?"

"I say take them out and get to it. No need in drawing out a fight."

"Pretty sure they're probably the first tier. We have no idea what's in store for us inside."

"This should have been under our jurisdiction."

"Well, that got all fucked up. And the Karysilans backed off."

"Only right that we handle our own mess."

"So," the other turned to his partner. "Broad daylight or cover of night?"

"It would take a good four hours to get to that server. Another two for the confirmation to clear."

"Broad daylight it is. Time?"

"When everyone gets off work. The less civilians, the better."

"Tomorrow?"

"Let's wait one more day."

He showed his partner the message from Emerson on his phone.

"Good. That gives us time to check out those eateries around the perimeter."

"Why is it always about food?"

"Because we're always hungry."

"That's the one drawback I hate about having alien DNA put in me."

They crawled backwards until only the top of the monolith was visible then double timed it back to their vehicle below.

In a fusion restaurant on the west side of the monolith, they sat in a back booth going over a hologram of the lower interior. The nerve center where the server was located laid ten floors below the main level. Intel suggested approximately twenty armed guards down there. It would be a massacre once they engaged. Whenever waitstaff came around, they would darken the image so no one could see. Off to the other side in the main dining room, sat a couple who seemed to have no intention of leaving. Their food was half eaten, they would take a few bites here and there, and the wine kept coming. The fake laughter and hushed talk screamed spy.

More watchers.

"Paranoid much?"

"Well, they do know we are trying to take away their power over this sector."

The food came, and they ate in silence for a few minutes before resuming their plans.

Four PM - March

From their vantage point above, the two agents aimed their weapons down towards the watchers. Similar to an AR15, the guns were light weight and could hold a charging clip good for one hundred rounds. The difference was the fire power and range. An advanced sniper, it was fresh off the assembly line. The first agent targeted the North and East side while his partner had the West and South. Workers filed out of the surrounding buildings, their day at the office over. It became a trickle in less than fifteen minutes signaling each place was practically empty. With the sun shining on a partly cloudy day and a minimal breeze that would barely alter trajectory, the two agents commenced their mission.

On the North side, one of the watchers sat at a café's outdoor table reading his tablet when the laser shot hit him. His head instantly slammed down onto the table top. The female watcher on her phone pacing dropped in a heap on the sidewalk and the man sipping his drink barely had time to notice before he too went down. Four seconds. The same happened with the watchers in each section.

The two agents jumped down to the bottom of the monolith and upon landing sped through the doors. Security was already on alert and a horde of them came rushing forward. The first agent stopped cold and laid a barrage of laser fire at them while his partner headed for the control room. Those not mowed down scrambled for cover, but the rounds pierced everything in their path. The entire floor went dark. Emergency lights flickered on, distracting the guards, and the first agent caught up with his partner.

They made their way to the maintenance room and from there, found the crawlspace that would lead them down. Only two minutes had passed. Quick, down and dirty.

The new head of security, appointed by the government, came barging into the situation room. His red face and quivering bottom lip was almost comical to Neil, but he managed to hold back his laughter.

"What the fuck is going on? Why haven't you deployed your people?" He yelled.

"First," Neil replied calmly. "You were warned this was going to happen."

"And I made sure to beef up security since none of you were taking this seriously."

"Secondly," Neil continued. "I am not going to put my people in harm's way for your agenda."

"This is your mess we're cleaning up!" The head of security moved up close to his face. The Recruiter leaned away from him. "I want a unit deployed and the rats exterminated."

"You can go fuck yourself."

"What did you say?"

The head of security grew redder, his eyes nearly bulging out of their sockets.

"I think you forgot something."

"And, what's that?"

Neil wrapped a leg around the head of security's neck and leaned back until he had clearance to slam the man's face to the floor. He kept his foot on the man's head as he stood and looked down at him.

"I am not someone to toy with. You are nothing to me. We let you play in our house long enough."

He caught a glimpse of the head of security tapping a button on his smartphone. A shit eating grin spread across the man's face. It disappeared when Neil stomped in his head.

"You stupid man."

He heard a succession of clicks and looking up saw the government personnel pointing their guns at him. There were five of them. His own people were rooted where they were, waiting for him to give an order. Killing them would bring more chaos and drama to the situation with the government demanding an answer and retribution. He contemplated for a moment if it was worth it.

"Lock them away," he ordered.

Confused, the government workers swung their weapons towards the nearest group of people, ready to fire. They weren't given the option. With lightning speed, his people disarmed and immobilized all five. Neil glanced at the head of security and let out a heavy sigh. Taking one arm by the wrist, he dragged the man out of the room following the others. Reinforcements would come within the next two hours. He hoped whoever had broken through arrived at their destination by then.

"Madam President," an aide called out from the doorway.

She turned towards him. The others in the room stopped talking.

"What is it?"

She frowned, knowing it was not good news.

The aide stepped further in and cleared his throat.

"It seems Grid city has been infiltrated. Our man in place at the monolith activated the call for assistance."

"God," she said slowly while making a fist, "Damn it!" She walked to the center of the room. "I want full tactical on the ground. No one leaves that area once we have it under control. And find those damn rodents before sunrise!"

"Yes, ma'am."

The aide left and everyone in the room kept silent. The president paced the room, one hand drumming fingers on her lips. Her initial response to the Grid city was to have military units deployed in each sector but her second in command advised against it due to how it would look. The citizens would ask too many questions as to why. Now, she had a fiasco on her hands and regretted putting her plan into play.

Dr. Bartley watched the vidscreen on his desk connected to the monolith mainframe. He had been informed of the infiltration and now awaited the transfer of control. The two men were inside the dark hub of the mainframe and standing on opposite sides of the control panel.

"Ready?" the first one asked.

The other nodded and tiny probes spewed from both mens' pores, slithering down into the components beneath. Their eyes glowed blue and the room became brighter. A series of codes filled the black cylinder in the center of the panel.

"On three," the second man said.

They counted silently, nodding to each other. Using their hand, they touched the send icon.

Professor Bartley saw his system reboot and a new one took its place.

"You had your chance. Now it's my turn," he said to the world.

A NEW ORDINANCE

Talbot stepped out of the black heavily tinted sedan and found himself in the heart of suburbia two states over. He took a look around the city square. Kitschy shops, high end accessories on passersby, and not a crappy outfit to be seen. Even the streets were old style stone, not paved, with a sign saying no motorized vehicles allowed. The sun was sloping down, and a slight breeze picked up. It was a perfect day for chaos.

A platform was being erected in the center for the festivities he had planned for later in the day. The sounds of pounding and drilling filled the square. People would be getting out of work or school soon and he expected a big turnout. Announcements had been sent out a week ago citing a town hall regarding Bi-Genetics. Stragglers slowed down out of curiosity as the uniformed soldiers made quick work of the scaffolding.

A man came out of the coffee shop across the way and he figured it was the owner. There was a scowl on the man's face as he approached the telepath. Some of the other business owners also came out, keeping an eye on the coffee shop guy to see what he was about to say or do.

"Good afternoon," the telepath greeted him. "Is there something you need?"

"How long is this," the man waved his hand in a circle around the area, "going to last?"

"Excuse me?"

"You heard me! This is disrupting our businesses, and for what? We don't care about those things in our city as long as they keep to themselves."

Talbot's eyes narrowed.

"We gave ample notice. If you were not prepared, then that is your own fault." He turned and walked away.

"You didn't answer my question."

In a split second, he was in front of the man, sharing the same breath. He watched the man's face contort into fear while the telepath whispered in his ear.

"I will not tolerate your tone. If you persist, you may find one or more of your limbs torn from your body." He backed off and continued towards the platform. "Have a good rest of your day. I look forward to seeing you at the town hall," he called out cheerily.

As he stood on the stage staring down at them his mind was made up about initiating phase three. There was no longer any doubt. He couldn't wait to get started. His earbud beeped, and he tapped it to answer.

"We're in position. Awaiting transport rendezvous." The male voice on the other end stated.

"Very good. Make sure there is a clear one-way exit."

"And, if we are met with resistance?"

"Don't kill anyone," he chided.

"Aside from that?"

"Don't kill," he reiterated, "anyone."

There was a long pause.

"Understood."

The call was disconnected, and he let out a loud sigh. It was going to get bloody.

At six o'clock, the city center was packed full of people already having arguments with each other. They went into a hush when a transport ship landed on the platform behind the podium and four men came out. The first two wore suits, the other a lab coat and the last out was a seemingly young man barely in his twenties, though his eyes said differently. One of the men in a suit was the telepath and he went up to the podium and adjusted the microphone. A handsfree one was usually brought to large events, but the telepath wanted it to look like an old school press conference. He tapped a few times to make sure it was on and began.

"Good evening citizens. As you know, there has been an epidemic of crimes against Bi-Genetics and their families. Due to this, new laws will need to be implemented."

"To hell with that!" An angry man in the crowd yelled.

Mumbles of concurrence swept through the masses.

"Yeah, why do we have to treat them special. No one wanted those Bi-ode freaks here anyway," another man said.

"They're abominations." A woman cried out.

"Last I checked, they were just as human as any of you," the scientist said. "This is why we have no right to ask the aliens to aide us."

"We never asked for their help and don't need it!"

The crowd became agitated and the speaker backed away from the podium to let the young man behind him come forth. Air swirled around his outstretched hands, gaining momentum and size until it was nearly his height. He unleashed it into the crowd, parting the center like the Red Sea, people falling to the wayside, knocking over their neighbors. His task complete, he walked back to his spot.

Talbot returned, leaning onto the podium.

"Are you done?" He addressed the frightened crowd. "Let's be civil, shall we?"

"The ones like him!" A man yelled.

"That's why we shouldn't…"

"He is rare among Bi-Genetics. How do you justify your thinking?"

The was a momentary silence. He took advantage of the situation.

"Since it is clear, your city has no intention for compliance, we will remedy it. All Bi-Genetics will be removed from the city. If need be, the entire family of said Bi-Genetics."

Looks of surprise and horror crossed every face and they seemed to struggle with that revelation. Some of them appeared to transition into anger.

Yes, who would you target for persecution in their steed? The telepath asked them silently.

"The operation has already commenced. It will go on until the entire region has been purged."

"Good riddance, then!" Someone shouted.

An awkward pause followed as no one else joined him. The implications were starting to already set in. The speaker turned away and headed back to the transport with the others behind him. He looked out the window as they lifted off to watch the people disperse.

This was only the beginning.

The bakery shop owner pulled into his driveway and found it blocked by a transport ship. From inside his house, he could hear yelling and screaming. Fumbling on the door release, he got it open and half ran towards the front door sitting wide open. As he neared the edge of the front lawn, he saw his teenage son being carried out like a sack over the shoulder of an orderly. Two men in suits had his wife by both arms as she tried to fight them off. Her face contorted in rage.

"You can't take him! He's not yours!" She screamed.

Another man in a suit came into view from the transport and stepped onto the porch.

"He was locked in a room with no lights and malnourished."

"I can do whatever I want to him! He's mine," she spat.

The baker stopped in his tracks. It was true, they treated their son like a prisoner whenever he wasn't in school to keep him out of sight. They didn't starve him, per se. He was fed enough to keep him going for the day. When he was born, they were so overjoyed. That turned sour when he was declared a Bi-Genetic at the age of seven. The thought of his son turning into a girl for the neighborhood boys to drag off and screw when they wanted made them both nauseous. Not having to deal with it was always something they wished for. Not like this.

"Let go of my wife!"

He went to free her and one of the men holding her kicked him back out the door. Tiny flashes of light swam around in his head as he stood. The man followed the orderly into the transport as the men in suits dropped his wife to do the same. Off in the distance, he saw another transport lift off from someone's yard. Strong wind blew him back down and he looked up at the one on his lawn take flight.

"This ain't right. They have no right," he whispered to himself.

Two hovercrafts descended on the lawn of a local attorney's home and he came running out to see what was going on. He shielded his face from the air shipping about and stared up into the cockpit of the first. The tiny blinking bulb by the pilot's ear seemed strange until the craft got closer and he saw it was coming directly out from behind it.

Men in tactical gear flooded his front lawn and started yelling at him to move aside. He backed up to his doorway and tried to block it. The unit bulldozed him out of the way and invaded his home. He heard screaming and crying and got up to fight.

"I wouldn't advise that," Brian, dressed in a suit said. He turned to get a good look at him. "I see you are angry. Rest assured, we will take good care of your children."

On cue, his wife and three kids were being forcibly dragged out. His wife was holding on to their youngest with everything she had while the soldiers tried in vain to pry him from her.

"You are not taking my children! Over my dead body," he nodded to his wife. "and hers."

"This district is not favorable for them. We cannot not allow them to stay here."

"I don't give shit about this district or any other! Those are my children!"

The whirring of the hovercrafts finally went silent and the man in the suit stepped forward.

"Then you all must leave. No Bi-Genetic will be left in this city."

The men trying to get at the mother backed off. She slumped to the ground, clinging to her child who was bawling profusely. Her husband stood in defiance before Brian until he simply nodded.

"Good." He turned to the unit leader. "Pack it up and load them on the transport."

"Roger that, sir."

Brian straightened his jacket and headed back to his private transport.

This is way more fun.

⌒

In cities across the nation, homes were invaded and children snatched while their parents fought the system and lost. Entire communities became ghost towns as their population dwindle by nearly sixty percent. School wings were closed off due to not being used. Businesses stayed open out of desperation even though their places sat empty most days.

The mayor of one city sat in the back of his government vehicle deep in thought while his eyes caught glimpses of the deserted streets. He knew the crime rate against Bi-Genetics was high and had planned to find a resolution at some point. What the facilities created was, in his opinion, the worst remedy. Already, the economic impact was showing. Everywhere he looked, companies were understaffed, no one making enough money to pay their bills. Most of the events slotted for the summer had been scrapped.

His driver maneuvered the vehicle in front of city hall and turned towards him.

"You need me to stick around, sir?" He nodded up at the stairs where an angry mob waited. "In case you want to get out fast."

"No. I have to take my lumps and like it."

"This isn't your fault, sir."

"Thanks. But, I know I'm partly to blame."

He opened the door and got out. Four bodyguards positioned themselves behind him. With a few deep breaths under his belt, he braved the crowd and went head first into the fray. His guards pushed people out of his path all the way to the doors. Inside wasn't much better. After going through security and into the assembly hall, he encountered a second smaller group of constituents with violent expressions.

"Time to face the music," he said to himself.

The din of voices talking over each other, arguing about the predicament the city found itself in made his head hurt. He pinched the bridge of his nose in frustration, squeezing his eyes shut. It was as if they had forgotten how it all came about.

"Why didn't you stop this?" Someone yelled.

"They came and kidnapped my kids by force!" A cried. "Look at the bruises they left on me!" She held up her bare arms to show defensive wounds.

"I had to let the employees that stayed go because I can't pay them." Another man said.

The Mayor sat straight and stared at them incredulous. He decided to remind them.

"Did many of you not make demands of my office to find someplace else to put them? That they should have been killed as babies? Or, what was the other thing? They shouldn't be allowed to go to school with your children because they'll get raped for the simple fact that you don't know how to raise your boys not to do such a thing?" He leaned forward, his teeth clenched. "None of you deserved to have those children. You brought this all on yourselves!"

He looked out at the horror-stricken faces in the assembly and knew he had hit a nerve. Not one person could deny his words. At some point, the silence was too great, and he signaled the moderator to end the town hall.

"Thank you, everyone for coming. Please follow security to the exit. Have a good evening."

A woman turned to him.

"We won't have a 'good' evening, you bastard!"

Tears welled up in her eyes as she left.

When the room was empty, the moderator came to stand by the mayor.

"Are you alright?"

"Hell no, I'm not alright! My city is falling into ruin."
His hands balled up on his thighs.

"Maybe they'll be willing to negotiate in a few months."

"We may not last that long."

⌒

President Lynmore paced the floor, chewing on her thumb nail. A habit she had quit in her college years now resurfaced. Her authority and pride were usurped by the Facilities' take over and there seemed to be no way out. The legislation appeared to be iron clad. All the Facility leaders declined her invitation to talk about it. A third of the country was declared in a state of emergency as their financial system collapsed.

Midafternoon sunlight made its way around the corner and spread through the oval office, making the blue in the carpet more pronounced. She stared down at the emblem, a symbol for the United States of America.

"I've failed my country."

Her assistants, George, and the Vice President looked up from their tablets and stared at her. She was visibly distressed and feeling at a loss. Vice President got up from his seat and went to stand by her.

"You have done no such thing. We were blindsided."

"You can't blame them for doing it, though," George said.

Heavy bags were under his eyes and his hair was unkempt. Nearly everyone in the room had been pulling all-nighters since the takeover.

"This was a bit too heavy handed," Vice President said. "There had to be a better way."

"I'm sure every district in the nation is saying the exact same thing." George also got up and stretched upwards, letting out a loud sigh. "We just didn't protect Bi-Genetics like we should have. They are the driving force of our upcoming battle and we're killing them off one by one."

The president turned on him, seething. "That's not true!" She backed away, scared of her own outburst and sat at her desk. "We needed more time."

"Which we don't have."

"They can't just ignore us," one of her assistants stated. "The survival of humanity is at stake."

"Exactly." George made eye contact with everyone to reiterate his point.

The Facility chairman swung back and forth in his seat as he stared at the giant vidscreen stream a slew of communications from various government agencies pleading for an audience. It had only been a little over two months and everyone was in panic mode. He felt it was not long enough for them to realize their errors. The civilized world needed to know the true meaning of financial pain. A devious smile spread across his lips.

The telepath entered the room and stopped to look at the screen. He too was undaunted by the desperation in the messages. Setting his bag on the nearest empty seat, he walked over to the facility leader and leaned on the table with one arm.

"Would you like to see the footage from the recent purge?" He asked.

"If I must. They all react the same, don't they? Indignation and assuming victimization."

"I find it amusing."

"It's disgusting!" The chairman snapped. His forehead furrowed.

"So, how long do we let the stew in their own sewage?"

The chairman's gaze was menacing.

"Oh, I'd say at least a year. Get it all nice and ripe until they can't stand the smell."

SHORT REPRIEVE

Crime plummeted in record numbers and speed as communities around the world began to feel the impact of Bi-Genetics being absent. Each facility had blocked themselves off from society, creating their own bubbles. Cities once rich with culture and revenue were dilapidated and short on funds. The strain was too great. Professor Bartley had touched base with the chairman and they agreed ten months was enough.

General Perrara sat in a transport with President Lynmore, the Secretary of Homeland Security, and Captain Darnizva. They landed at the Shadow Organization's base in the desert. Hana greeted them along with Scott.

"Good to see you," Hana said to Darnizva. "And welcome, Madam President, Homeland Secretary." She bowed low in traditional Asian fashion. Her gaze fell on General Perrara. "General, you look well."

"Don't lie to me," he said. "I earned these bags under my eyes."

In truth, they all looked worse for wear. Perrara hoped they could get to the bottom of the whole Bi-Genetic fiasco before the day was over.

"This way," Hana said. "Our other guests await."

The President tensed up and Perrara realized she had never met the four aliens. He eyed the Homeland Secretary acting nervous. Hana led them to a conference room on one the upper levels and used the biometric scan to open it. Inside, Celestial Mother, her mate, and the two Chombrazen warriors lounged in their seats. Along with them was a representative from the major countries. The theater seating was circular to allow everyone to see each other. There was a podium in the center and four chairs, two on each side.

"Well." Perrara walked down to the seat with his name on it. "Let's get this show started."

Once everyone was seated, the Facility chairman, the telepath, and two scientists entered the center. Perrara sucked in his breath at the sight of the telepath. The man looked up at him and winked.

"You know him?" George asked.

"I don't want to, but yes."

The Facility chairman went to the podium.

"I'm sure you all know why you're here."

"Because you decided to force a worldwide economic collapse," one of the world leaders yelled out.

"No. My concern was for the Bi-Genetic population."

"And you sacrificed humans to further their agenda," another leader spoke.

"Oh, good God!" President Lynmore said. "Have none of you learn nothing?"

The room got quiet and Darnizva rested an arm on the back of his chair.

"This is what I was afraid of."

"As did we," the chairman added. "Have you all forgotten why we need more Bi-Genetics?"

Looks of guilt and pain were noticeable around the room.

"Your time is nearly up," Celestial Mother said. "We have done all we can to try and steer your race onto the right course. I am inclined to rescind my offer."

"As you should," Darnizva stated.

"I cannot blame you on this."

"Wait!" A world leader cried out. "Not all of us are so narrow minded to think we can survive on our own. Please, do not give up on us yet."

The chairman ceded the podium to one of the scientists.

"In order to stay on track, the third generation Bi-Genetics must be trained and ready. Many of them are still in teen years, some younger. All in the care of the facilities." The mood went grim. "I am proposing a restart of the Primer system to increase numbers."

That sent the room in an uproar. Leaders began shouting.

"Growing humans in tubes at accelerated rates was a shameful catastrophe!"

"How could you think to bring something like that back up?"

"Have you lost your sense of humanity as well?"

Talbot leaned back and stared at them all before his eyes turned to burning hot pools of blue. He sent one word to them.

Silence.

They all held their heads at the psychic attack. George wiped blood from his ears and stared at Perrara in astonishment. Perrara used his fingers to pinch blood off his nose. President Lynmore sat horrified, blood seeping from the corners of her eyes.

"Are we done?" The chairman asked as the noise diminished.

Celestial Mother was out of her seat.

"You've been holding out on me. Why wasn't I given that one?" She pointed to the telepath.

"This is not the time. We need to discuss the issue at hand."

She stepped down, the sound of her boot striking the

floor echoed. The world leaders closest to her looked up in terror at her size and expression.

"I care not for your society and politics. I am here to train your fragile bodies."

"Please," Darnizva said. He glanced over at her.

"Very well. I will wait. But, he is mine when this is over."

Talbot went pale, not liking what he was about to be traded to or for.

"Will we get our people back?" President Lynmore asked. Her voice was shaky, her body still feeling the effects of the telepath.

"The conditions must be met, and new laws implemented before we start releasing them into your care. And then, it will be on a voluntary basis. If they do not want to return, we will not force them."

"Agreed," a world leader said.

A loud beep broke the somber atmosphere and Darnizva touched the commlink on his wrist. He read the message and frowned.

"What is it?" Perrara asked, concerned.

"Good tidings, humans. The Relliance is in the middle of a political snafu and are giving you an extra two years."

"Two years!" President Lynmore said. "That's not much of a reprieve."

"It's better than nothing at all," Hana whispered. "We're not ready."

"Then, I suppose we better straighten our asses out and get with the program, no?" A world leader asked.

The aliens in the room gave each other a knowing look. Humans were on a road to extinction if they didn't.

END

EXCERPT FROM

CURVE OF HUMANITY
BOOK FOUR

CRIPPLED EARTH

INNOVATION

Quelly Riggs was going to be late for lab, again. This would be the third time in one semester and the professor was getting a little irate. She ran haphazardly down the hall, white lab coat held tight between one elbow while she tried to tie her thick black curly hair into a messy updo and get her right shoe on correctly. She could feel her sock bunching underneath the arch of her foot.

She thought back to her college days when she worked for the Shadowman Organization. The group went to extremes to get equality for Bi-Genetics. Although the project was a success, too many people had been murdered in its name. There were a few regrets but all the same, would have done it again.

Her current residency would get her one step closer to becoming a professor and right now she felt her own self in the way. She was on to something big with the new secret project she was working on. It just needed another year or so of testing. Being in the science field had become cut throat since the alien crash landings. The applicants aspiring to be the next great scientist exploded within ten years and even more so after it was announced, in secret of course, that a way to evacuate Earth was needed. All ideas were said to be on the table yet the extreme ones were tossed.

Bursting into the lab, she was confronted by every-one turning to the doors as the professor stopped talking

241

and did the same. His eyes narrowed in anger and he said nothing, except point to her seat and resume his lecture. Quelly, standing like a rooted tree out of embarrassment, heard chuckling from both sides of the room. She walked hurriedly to her seat and got out her tablet. The person next to her made tsk sounds and he looked her up and down with disgust. Now that was uncalled for. Getting her stylus, she started taking notes.

The great thing about being in the scientists' elite club was that you got a huge suite with a private lab attached on the back end. The military felt it a necessary amenity to keep the scientists in the zone of creativity. Many of the residents figured it was an excuse to keep them on a short leash. Quelly didn't mind one bit. Not having to commute to the facility labs meant she was able to work on her own without interference.

She walked over to the test specimen and took a reading from the monitors hooked up to it. The clear gelatinous substance was shimmying a bit. That meant it wasn't going to remain stable. Previous specimens had done the same except this time, it lasted three months. She was sure it would liquefy within the next few days.

"Damn it," she swore softly to herself, pacing the lab deep in thought. It was an improvement though still not there yet. She needed it to remain stable for years, not months and so far had not found the right combination of chemicals to produce her results.

"Come on, girl. Think. What's missing?"

She went over to the desk and caught a glimpse of herself in the mirror. All candidates had to have alien DNA introduced in their system to slow down aging and increase longevity. College came after four years in the U.S. Navy and she was a little rough around the edges in looks. Being around other young students helped her get that together and now at age thirty five, she didn't look a day past her twenties.

A timer beeped by the mini cryochamber she had acquired years ago. She went over and put on her gloves to remove the next specimen. With long black gloves that went up to her shoulders, she carefully grabbed it and placed it in a holding container next to the other one. The specimen resembled a block of dry ice. When the mist cleared, it was like a crystal. Quelly frowned as she shut the door and secured the latch.

Once stabilized, she could then work on a destabilizer for it. One step at a time. She had two more years before her residency was up. Even if her idea didn't save the human race, at least she'd know she accomplished something.

∽

So it's come to this.

The Joint President of the United States thought to himself, sitting down in the nearly empty conference room. All the world leaders had decided to do video face to face instead of in real life. No one wanted to leave their country unattended while they each tried to push their scientific communities to find a solution to the evacuation problem. A meeting with the high officers of the League was scheduled for the day and he was informed only an hour ago that only Commander Ammordia and Darnizva would be present. President Lynmore was in no mood for more bad news and instructed him to go in her steed.

With Earth headed towards annihilation, the United States had become the center of attention in a bad way. After the grid city debacle, a two president system was introduced to alleviate the pressure and duties of the position. He had been voted in unanimously and without his knowledge. The last thing he wanted was the responsibility of an entire nation on his shoulders.

"Sir." Secretary Regis, ageless from the days of the crash landing, slid in the seat next to him and set her tablet down. "We will find a way. If we don't…then it was meant to be. A lot of religious leaders are saying it is the rapture and the apocalypse all rolled into one."

"I am not going to lay down and give up!" He seethed. "Not yet! Not without a knock down drag out fight." The wall of video screens in front of them flickered on right as his Vice President sauntered in. She took her place opposite the Joint President and they all waited for the world leaders to be present. "Humanity cannot come to a screeching halt. Not like this."

Two separate screens located on either side of the room came to life with Ammordia on one and Darnizva on the other. Seeing the Captain, the President felt a twinge of heartache. The young soldier looked exhausted, and not optimistic. Learning all the details a few years back gave him a clearer picture of what they were actually up against.

"Is everyone accounted for?" Ammordia asked. Heads bobbed in acknowledgement. "Good. Let's get started." An image of a solar system, clearly not theirs, replaced hers and she began to explain.

"During the research my technicians conducted, they came across a solar system not too far away and may be capable of sustaining human life. A rough analysis was prepared but you can't really know unless a human goes there." She turned to Darnizva's monitor.

"Given the data and location of the planets in that solar system, it is estimated to take about ten years to arrive there."

"In our spaceships?" The Russian President inquired.

"No. In one of ours. Your ships, though far more advanced than fifty years ago, is not capable of traveling at the speeds we can."

"Are we really so far behind in our technology?" The leader of China protested.

"I'm afraid the answer is yes." Dour faces became prevalent across the screens. "It is not anything to be ashamed of. Every civilization has to go through an evolutionary stage."

"But, we are about to get wiped out before we can even realize our potential." The Joint President stated in defeat. He heard Regis squirm in her seat. "Now, with less than twenty years before the deadline, we can't afford to send someone out there and back to report their findings."

"The timeline just won't work," The Russian President added.

Darnizva was at a loss and he struggled to keep his composure. His hands were shaking and he couldn't understand why. He had been in countless battles and saw much bloodshed. This feeling of helplessness was something he did not like. He looked up at Ammordia, who was back onscreen.

"Mother." Ammordia's lips pursed. The President's, along with everyone else's, eyes went wide and they all focused on her image. "He won't help me, will he?"

"Your father is the General of the League. He has more pressing matters to deal with and returned to Karysilan to go over strategies for retaliation. The aftermath of the last battle was not for the weak of heart. Your brother..." Darnizva shook his head violently. "His wounds were too great. I should have told you before but you too had a lot to deal with." Ammordia's facial expression sagged and she looked ill. "We were able to use most of his tissue to regenerate a new body but we won't know if it was a success for a few years more."

Darnizva merely nodded and clamped his mouth shut painfully tight. He didn't regret saving his squadron, but the outcome ended up being a greater burden than he could have ever imagined. What happened after he jumped was a mystery to him and he felt guilty for not inquiring about the rest of the command ships he left to continue the fight.

"I understand," he finally responded. "Thank you, Commander Ammordia," he said in a formal tone.

"Darnizva…"

"I will take it from here."

He gave her a defiant look and they locked eyes before she nodded in agreement and terminated her feed. Knowing he was visibly shaken, he mustered all the energy he had and straightened his posture. He stared at the many human faces on vidscreens before him and made a decision.

"I have a ship that can exceed even our fighter's speed. I will send a reconnaissance troop to the solar system and do some research. They can make it back within fifteen years."

"That only gives us five years to try and get everyone who wants to go, off Earth," the French President said in a panic.

"I understand. That is the best solution at this junction."

"Well you're going to have to better than that!" The President of China snapped.

"I don't think we have the luxury of kicking a gift horse in the mouth here," the Joint President stated.

Everyone clammed up in hostile humiliation for they all knew it was true and better than anything they were capable of doing in the next twenty odd years. After that was said, many of the world leaders terminated their feeds out of frustration and clear embarrassment.

"Well, I guess that is all we need to know for today, isn't it?" The Joint President said leaning back in his chair. "I thank you all for your time." The rest of the vidscreens went black leaving Darnizva still sitting in a daze contemplating something. "What are you thinking, Captain?"

"That I should have been able to do more sooner."

"Oh, no you don't!" Regis snapped at him, causing him to jerk his head up in her direction. "This was an accident. Tragic, yes, but never the less, an accident. You can't rely on your parents to bail you out at every turn. This is war. Suck it up!"

Darnizva stepped back in shock at her words which stung as they hit home. He was not a child anymore at the ripe age of one hundred and ninety four. Still far too young to have his own squadron yet seasoned enough to know when to draw the line in the sand. Regaining his composure, he wiped his face.

"You are correct. I apologize for being childish just now. I will get on with my plan. Please coordinate with the Commander Fleet leader on battle strategy. For humans twenty years may seem long but to us, in a battle, it's a blink of an eye."

"Will do, Captain. Good luck." Vice President offered.

"You too." Darnizva terminated his feed.

"Well, Mr. President?" His Vice President inquired.

"Let's pray for a miracle."

"There were only a handful who declined."

"So, we're ready for phase one?"

"Getting the packets together as we speak. Hana is very resourceful."

He saw a hint of possessiveness creep up in the professor's eyes.

"Yes, he is." There was pause. "What about the training grounds?"

"Still working out the kinks. The indoor assessment looks promising. I believe if even a handful get through that obstacle course, we would have a good unit on our hands."

"Yes, but we need a hell of lot more than that."

"Don't take me so literally, Professor," Perrara laughed.

It was true in sense. The course was built to put a strain on all the senses. One wrong decision and the candidate could get seriously hurt. He had two medical wings set up on either side to ensure quick response. But, the professor was right. They had to get as many units as possible to plant inside the military ranks.

"Phase Two?"

"Still waiting on Professor Bartlett."

He knew what the doctor had been through and cursed the scientist who created the facilities. A lot of horrors happened in those places. None of it for the greater good of humanity. This time, the Bi-Genetics on his list would suffer for one that does. Bartlett's hesitation was not surprising.

"He's meticulous. Give him all the time he needs. He knows the deadline."

"I'm just anxious," Professor Makoto snapped.

"So am I. Let's have a little more patience."

Professor Makoto nodded.

"I hope to hear an update soon."

With that, the screen went blank and his screen saver resumed. General Perrara sighed and swung around in his chair to face the window. Night had fallen and the desert sky was full of stars. Mankind wanted so badly to reach further than their solar system but knowing what's out there, he wondered if that was the right answer. Compared to the aliens in their midst, humans were like insects. And not the resourceful kind.

Can we even win?

ABOUT THE AUTHOR

Hi there. I'm Maquel A. Jacob. I have had a passion for the written word since the age of seven, reading everything I could get my grubby little hands on which included encyclopedias and the thesaurus. At twelve, I had my first encounter with a Stephen King novel and was hooked. I then became inspired to write my own brand of fiction. Combining multiple genres to keep things interesting.

I am a HUGE Anime fan, love a great bottle of wine and rock out to heavy metal music. Green and lush Oregon is where I currently reside spinning imaginary worlds in my head and daydreaming.

For cool limited-edition Swag, updates, FREE short stories, Newsletters

...and more

Visit: http://www.maquelajacob.com/

Like Maquel A. Jacob on Facebook, Tumblr and Twitter

@MaquelAJ1

Also find me on Goodreads

MAJart Works is on Instagram

www.ingramcontent.com/pod-product-compliance
Lightning Source LLC
Chambersburg PA
CBHW021006120726
47905CB00009B/2880